The Journey of A Shepherd's Wife

The Journey of A Shepherd's Wife

Virginia Cooper Stokes

ReadersMagnet, LLC

The Journey of a Shepherd's Wife
Copyright © 2018 by Virginia Cooper Stokes

Published in the United States of America
ISBN Paperback: 978-1-947765-92-4
ISBN Hardback: 978-1-948864-33-6
ISBN eBook: 978-1-947765-93-1

All rights reserved. No part of this publication may be reproduced, stored in a retrieval system or transmitted in any way by any means, electronic, mechanical, photocopy, recording or otherwise without the prior permission of the author except as provided by USA copyright law.

No lines, parts, and quotations were taken from other books or any previous publications.

The opinions expressed by the author are not necessarily those of ReadersMagnet, LLC.

ReadersMagnet, LLC
10620 Treena Street, Suite 230 | San Diego, California, 92131 USA
1.619.354.2643 | www.readersmagnet.com

Book design copyright © 2018 by ReadersMagnet, LLC. All rights reserved.
Cover design by Ericka Walker
Interior design by Shieldon Watson

DEDICATION OF THIS BOOK

To My Husband, Tom
Children
David And Debra
And
In Memory Of My Beloved Parents
John And Ruthella Cooper
And
My Youngest Brother, Tim

Table of Contents

Preface 9
Introduction 11

PART I
God's Calling And Our Ministries

Chapter 1　　Growing Up 15
Chapter 2　　When You Yield, God Works 19
Chapter 3　　Grandmother's Ring 23
Chapter 4　　The Brush Arbor Meeting 27
Chapter 5　　The Tornadoes 31
Chapter 6　　He Came Back 35
Chapter 7　　The Loving Church 37
Chapter 8　　Staff Friends In The Ministry 41
Chapter 9　　Things Are Not Always What They Seem 45
Chapter 10　Life On Doty Creek 51
Chapter 11　Lessons From Job 55
Chapter 12　Pride 59
Chapter 13　God's Will 63

PART II
Experiences And Lessons Of Life

Chapter 14　Not A Chance 69
Chapter 15　The Ends Do Not Justify The Means 73
Chapter 16　Provisions 77

Chapter 17	Talents	81
Chapter 18	Marriage	83
Chapter 19	Parenthood	85
Chapter 20	Gossip And Rumors	89
Chapter 21	Kay	91
Chapter 22	McAdoo	93
Chapter 23	Laughter In The Church	95
Chapter 24	Worship	99
Chapter 25	Living In The Parsonage	101
Chapter 26	Working Outside Of The Church	103
Chapter 27	Ministers' And Wife's Conference	105
Chapter 28	Gone Fishing	107
Chapter 29	Too Much Talking	109
Chapter 30	Foot Washing	111
Chapter 31	Expedient	113
Chapter 32	Insight At The Water Park	115
Chapter 33	The Pastor's Study	117
Chapter 34	Other Friends In The Ministry	119
Chapter 35	Going Home	123
Chapter 36	Cancer	125
Chapter 37	Love Returned	129
Chapter 38	Family	135
Chapter 39	Living And Dying	137
Chapter 40	Patience	141
Chapter 41	The Grace Of God	147
Chapter 42	My Prayer For The Church Member	149
Chapter 43	My Prayer For The Minister's Wife	151
Chapter 44	The Final Chapter	155

Preface

Exodus tells the story of the Israelites leaving their known homes in Egypt to experience God in a new land without knowing what to expect. In *The Journey of a Shepherd's Wife*, Virginia Cooper Stokes relates her family's personal exodus to experience God as a clergy family and wander into the unknown territories spiritually and physically in the commonwealth of Kentucky.

Just as Aaron and Hur held up the hands of Moses in battle in Exodus 17:12, the pastor's wife is called to hold up the shepherd's hands. She is to be a helpmate to help her husband, encourage and stand beside him, as well as to use the gifts God has given her in the ministry.

Virginia has given a glimpse of life in a parsonage by being transparent in how the Lord teaches each of us on the journey. She truly exemplifies a person of grace and "helping hands". In sharing the insights along the journey, she is willing to expose her personal growth to be a blessing to others.

I wish this book had been written before my husband and I started out in the ministry! Insights in this book, would help other clergy couples.

This journey began in prayer, was sustained in prayer and continues in prayer. To God be the glory!

—Glenda Myers, pastor's wife, Gainsville, GA

Introduction

As a child, at church, I would watch my minister's wife. She was pretty, had three children who were always well-dressed and very well-behaved. She was sophisticated, always had a smile on her face and dressed stylishly. She appeared to not have a worry in the world. The church seemed to never have a problem. No one ever spoke of any dissension. It appeared to be the perfect church, but I was looking through the eyes of a child.

Before I married my minister husband, Tom, I felt the calling to be a pastor's wife. The pastor is a shepherd. He guides, leads, and takes care of his flock. I embraced the calling to support my husband and to love the people that we were to minister with and in the communities in which we would live.

At times my idealistic view of the position changed. Especially when there were problems in the church and the children came along. Sometimes I questioned, was it supposed to be like this? What was I doing wrong? Where are you, Lord?

For forty-five years, God has revealed to me thoughts and insights of this calling. Through many ups and downs, God has always been there and brought us through. The names of the churches that we have served are not important. Some people's names have been changed; in no way do I want to embarrass anyone. The important things are the lessons learned; our spiritual growth, learning to depend on the Lord and seeing Him work in our lives as well as other people's.

Most people can relate to some of the real life stories that I am sharing with you. We all have our unique experiences as we walk with Christ. It has been an exciting journey and at times hard for me to realize that some things really happened. I have learned that these struggles and trials have been blessings in disguise.

PART I

God's Calling And Our Ministries

Chapter 1

Growing Up

I WAS RAISED ON a farm in Gallatin, Tennessee. There were five children, four boys and me. Mother, daddy and my father's mother made up our family. Grandma was our only living grandparent. The other three had died and we never got to know them. We also had a dairy and the cows had to be milked morning and evening.

It looked like the middle of the night when mother came into my room to wake me. Life on a dairy farm meant getting up before the chickens. As the only daughter in the family I usually didn't have to help milk the cows. That was the job for my dad and brothers. For all to get fed breakfast, mother needed my help in the kitchen. It was always hard to get my eyes open that time of the day, but I did like helping mother. So while the "menfolk" were at the milking barn, mother and I were working hard to have breakfast on the table when they got back to the house. This was the routine especially during the school year.

On Sundays, we had a little more time. After milking was completed, daddy had to leave for work. Besides the farm, he worked full time for the TVA. Working three out of four Sundays was his schedule. This bothered our father because he loved his church and hated that he couldn't go but once a month on Sunday morning. He always attended on Sunday and Wednesday nights.

Mother could not drive a car. Even if she had a license she would not have been able to leave because she cared for our grandmother. We walked to the end of our lane and Miss Lucy would pick us up, take us to church and back home after the service. On Sunday nights daddy taught training union. He would take us to church. There was no arguing about going, it was expected of us. Johnny, my oldest brother, and I were saved at a fall revival and joined First Baptist Church of Gallatin, Tennessee when I was ten years old. Our parents taught us about tithing, missions and living the Christian life by example.

In addition to mother's regular duties as wife, mother of five and caring for our grandmother, she was very involved with the 4-H Club and Boy Scout projects with her children and others. We were taught by example and instruction to work hard; but we also had our time to play and be with children who were our neighbors. Mother seemed to be the glue that held everything together in our family. She was like a "foreman" who kept everyone on track with chores and getting to our activities on time.

Daddy was a hard-working, humble man who always had time for his family and for anyone else that he came in contact with. We had "hands" to help us during tobacco cutting time and hay bailing. Daddy paid for their labor, but he also helped out many of these families when in need. He loved the Lord and lived his convictions with his dealings with people. He was known for his honesty, giving and love.

Our grandmother, dad's mom, was not at all like our father. She was not a very nice person. Everything had to be about her and what she wanted. Several times the neighbors would call and come by to borrow a cup of sugar, flour, etc. She would run them off and we would go out the back door and take them what they needed. Our father was her only child. She thought that the boys were "ok" but she did not like me. She always seemed to hold it against me that I was a girl. Not that I could do anything about that. Sometimes she would give the boys things. Only once did she give me something, and even then she took it back right away.

Most of my childhood memories were pleasant and filled with laughter. It was fun living on the farm with the boys and neighbors our age to play with. Most of the negative memories that I have relate to my grandmother.

One of my worse memories of my childhood Christmases was one time that she deliberately excluded me. When Mother and daddy were going Christmas shopping, she asked Mother to get a basket of fruit, candy and trinkets from the store for Christmas presents for us. She put the boys' names on the basket she fixed, but left mine off. I still remember running into the other room, hiding behind the door and crying with a broken heart. I received other presents that year from my parents and my brothers; but the only present I had really wanted was for her to acknowledge me as one of her grandchildren.

As the years passed and she became increasingly feebler, I continued to do things for her and try to get her approval. Things were fine as long as my parents were near me, but when they were out of the room, she would degrade my looks or how I dressed. Mother and daddy tried to talk to her and get her to treat me better. Her health continued to worsen. I would worry about her especially when she was sick and in the hospital. For years she remained in a hospital bed, slowly losing her memory. At times, mother got a short break when grandma was in the hospital or stayed in the nursing home. No matter where she was, I never stopped trying to get her approval and love but that never happened. I spent those years wondering what I had done to make her dislike me and why I did not deserve her love.

Chapter 2

When You Yield, God Works

My years in high school were fun. I was in the marching and concert band all four years of high school. I never missed a football game in four years in high school, and I still don't know much about the game. I was too busy visiting with others while the games were going on. I excelled in 4-H club with many wins and possibilities for the future.

My junior year was a time of decision for plans after high school. All juniors were scheduled to see the high school counselor to discuss future plans. I was an average student, some A's, B's and C's. I worked very hard to get the grades that I received. Part of the problem was that I never did well on tests. The counselor told me that she did not think that I would make it in college. The best thing for me was to get married, have children or maybe work at a local department store. That was not what I wanted to hear. I don't think that she intended to motivate me, but she did. From that time on I was determined to do more with my life. There was nothing wrong with getting married and having children, but she acted like I was not capable of doing anything else. At times my grandmother's discouraging words would also ring in my ears. I did not know what my future held but I had the assurance that God wanted me to further my education.

During the summer before my senior year I attended a retreat in Ridgecrest, North Carolina. Several missionaries spoke during the week. On the last night a missionary couple spoke. They had been missionaries to what was then the country of Rhodesia. After hearing them speak of their work and the great needs around the world, I walked the aisle and gave myself to full time Christian service. I had been a Christian for years, but this was an extension of my Christian calling. At that time I did not know where that calling would lead.

I was counseled about my decision. The same missionary wife spoke with and prayed with me. She shared her favorite Bible verses from Proverbs 3: 5–6. "Trust in the Lord with all of thine heart and lean not on your own understanding; in all your ways acknowledge him and he shall make your path straight" (NIV). I have never forgotten those words and many times they were the exact words that I needed for encouragement. After graduation I decided to attend a Christian college and was accepted at Belmont College in Nashville, Tennessee.

The summer before the fall semester, I won a state championship in 4-H club for Home Economics. During my freshman year at Belmont, I attended a national competition and was a national runner-up. I was offered a scholarship to the University of Tennessee in Home Economics. It was flattering, but I turned it down. I did not feel that was the field that I was called to go into and not the college to attend.

I stayed at Belmont and graduated after four years with a major in Psychology and minor in Sociology. Both studies were interesting to me and I felt that I had a better grasp on people and needs. I had no problems getting through college, matter of fact, my grades were better in college than in high school. I remembered the high school counselor. When I graduated, for a brief moment, I wanted to go back to my high school, stick the degree in her face and say "you were wrong."

While in college, I worked for the Psychology Department. An elderly lady that I had the privilege of working with helped me get a job at the Baptist Sunday School Board (Lifeway). I became a research assistant. I met Lynn. She and I became the first female researchers. It was a challenge, because some of the men did not accept us. Some did not think that women were capable of holding similar jobs. Most of the department was wonderful to us. We had the opportunity to travel over the United States, meet people, and complete surveys in churches. My thoughts remained on my calling. I thought about going on to seminary, but I had a great salary and the job was secure or that was what I thought.

After two years, several departments at the Sunday School Board were downsized. Our department was part of the cutbacks. The last six jobs filled in my department were deleted. Mine was one of those jobs. I was offered another job, to supervise a group of ladies in a typing pool. The job did not interest me. We were given six month's severance pay. The money that I received afforded me the opportunity to go to seminary. I chose and was accepted at Southern Seminary in Louisville, Kentucky. I felt that God was making a way for me to fulfill my calling. After those two years of spiritual searching I came to the conclusion that my calling was to be involved in missions as a minister's wife. I wanted to study Social Work and I thought that the best place to meet a minister was in seminary. So, I packed my bags and off I went.

I arrived at Southern Seminary on August 15, 1971. On September 30, 1971 I attended a supper and fellowship for all dorm students on campus. I had just gotten back from seeing the doctor for a sinus infection. I felt and looked awful and really did not want to attend but one of the other students talked me into going. The girls from my dorm were sitting around a table when some of the male students introduced themselves and asked to sit with us. All the guys were theology students. I introduced myself and said that I was a social work major. Tom Stokes looked over to me and said "so you are one of those irreligious ones." He was kidding, but I did not know how to take him. Later that night I saw him again and he asked me on a date.

Our second date was on a Sunday. Tom was the pastor of a country church outside of Salem, Indiana. He took me with him to his church. On the way there he told me that the church did not have any indoor bathrooms. I still did not know how to take him and thought that he was kidding. I had never gone to a church without an indoor bathroom. Sure enough, the church had two outhouses located out in a field in back of the church. After church we had a picnic in a field owned by one of his church members. It was a beautiful sunny fall day with the birds chirping. The cows were grazing in the field next to us. Then a farmer started spreading manure in another field nearby. Being a country girl, I felt right at home.

After two dates we both knew that we were meant to be together. It did take God's intervention, by losing my job, to give me the courage to go to seminary. Once I was given that opportunity, I took it and God worked. I received an engagement ring at Christmas. I started planning for our wedding. We set our wedding date for June 17, 1972.

Chapter 3

Grandmother's Ring

A MONTH BEFORE WE married, my grandmother died. The one thing that my grandmother had given me and took back was her engagement ring. Upon her death, my mother gave it back to me. I put it in my jewelry box and at the time did not think anything about it.

As the days grew closer to getting married, the more depressed I got. I had suffered some depression in college, but it would go away in a few days. The week before the wedding, I was almost a basket case. Since I was in seminary and away from home, mother did most of the planning for the wedding. Basically, all I had to do was attend wedding showers. I thought that I was having some jitters from all of the activities and that everything would be fine after the wedding.

Our wedding was on a beautiful warm Saturday afternoon. Friends and family from Seminary, Florida and Texas attended our wedding. Our parents had invested a lot of money and hard work to provide us with a wonderful wedding. My father was shaking and had tears in his eyes as he walked me down the aisle. He was losing his little girl but he willingly gave me away. I had tears in my eyes for another reason, but I did not know why. I was so depressed that I thought any minute I would die.

After the wedding, we took off on our honeymoon. We headed to Florida. Tom had told a first cousin that he would perform her wedding the next weekend. This was supposed to be the time of our lives. Tom did everything to help me with the depression, but it continued. He took me to a funny movie, I cried through the whole movie. I thought that when we got back to Louisville and the Seminary that everything would be alright. I was wrong.

We arrived back in Louisville. We house-sat that summer. The house was a large three story house. Tom went back to work. I did not work that summer nor would I have been able. I became afraid of almost everything. I became fearful of going up the steps to the upper levels of the house and would not go into the basement. The only place that I felt safe was on the main floor. Then I got to where I did not want to go outside. Things were not getting better. I loved Tom and I did not know what was happening to me. I had always been an adventuresome person and afraid of very little.

This was also a very difficult time for Tom. His love for me was evident. He did not know what was happening to me and did not know what to do. We decided that I needed to see a counselor. There was not a day that went by that I was not depressed. I even got to where I could not cry anymore. I never did consider taking my life, but just did not want to wake up in the mornings. I prayed that the Lord would take me in the night and I would not have to face another day. I was a Christian and I did not know what was happening. I prayed and prayed but was not getting any answers.

Tom was completing his Master of Theology degree. We decided to talk with Dr. Wayne Oates at the seminary to get an evaluation. He was extremely nice and showed concern. He thought that I needed to see a chaplain at Baptist East hospital in Louisville. I started seeing him weekly. Slowly, I could see that I was getting better and was able to start working. I applied and got a job in a large hospital as an assistant in the recreation department of the Psychiatric Ward. At that time that was rather appropriate, I surely could identify with the patients. However, when one of them had an ailment, I usually ended up with the same thing. I identified with the patients too much, but it did help me to know that was not the field of social work that I was suited.

I continued to see the chaplain every other week then once a month for a year. It took a lot of work on Tom and my part but it was worth every minute that I talked with the chaplain. When I look back, that was one of the best years of my life. It was a turning point.

He helped me see the root of my depression. It was my grandmother. My severe depression started when she died. No longer would I be able to get her love and approval. That threw me into feelings of hopelessness and fear for the future. Would this happen again with others that I shared love? My self-esteem had been damaged by her words of discouragement and rejection.

Slowly, I started to heal and understand the damage that a person can do to another. I had been clinically depressed. The most important thing was that the healing process started. God was working in my life to help me understand and accept the situation with my grandmother. Since that time, I have not suffered from clinical depression again. For several years I had short spells of depression, but never to the extreme that I had during those days. I learned how to deal with the depression. I also learned Christ's blood had made me whole and I was loved and accepted by Him.

I also learned that there is always an answer to our problems, hurts and situations. Sometimes the answers do not come easy or quick, but they will come if we persist and let God show us the way. He will surround us with people who care and help us through our difficulties.

I have heard people say that the first year of marriage was supposed to be one of the happiest times of your life. I could not say that ours was the happiest, but it did give us a good foundation of love and respect for each other, and a willingness to stick together through hard times. If it had not been for a loving husband, our commitment to each other and the Lord, our marriage might not have lasted.

One day I was looking into my jewelry box. I had forgotten about grandma's engagement ring. I took it out and put it on my left picky finger. I felt the need to wear it, maybe because it was the only thing I had that belonged to her.

Self-worth should not be measured according to others response to us. When we have done the best that we can, then we have to leave the situation up to God. Sometimes we see positive results and other times we don't. We are not accountable for others but only for ourselves. This is a hard lesson for Christians to accept because we want to be accepted and loved. We should continue to love even if that love is not received or given back. My ultimate goal is to please the one who saved me and called me to my ministry. As the years have gone by, I realized that I no longer needed to wear my grandmother's ring, so it is now forever in my jewelry box.

Chapter 4

The Brush Arbor Meeting

ABOUT A YEAR AFTER we married another church was interested in calling Tom as pastor. One weekend we went to the church to look over the situation. They were very interested for us to come and minister. We were still in seminary at the time and it would be a part-time ministry at first. After we moved to the area, the pay was to be increased.

I was raised in and loved the country but this church was 22 miles from anything. I was raised in a large church in a town that had all kinds of stores. The more I thought of moving to this rural area the more I decided that I did not want to go. One night I was at the seminary library. I was burdened, so I went outside, leaned up against a large column of the building and started praying. When the praying started I knew that was where we were going to minister.

We accepted the call and moved into the parsonage next to the church. After the call and shortly before we arrived the church had what they called a "Pentecostal split". A group in the church believed that a person was not saved unless they spoke in tongues.

This group split off and organized another church. Most of the church members were local and related to each other. So they were related to the people who split. Our first year was spent trying to help mend broken relationships. We visited the hospitals and in homes. The people loved for us to visit in their homes and eat a meal. We also met several of the people who had split from the church and became friends.

The split-off group was having a Brush Arbor meeting. Several had asked us to attend their meetings. I had never heard of a Brush Arbor meeting. They explained to me that it was a series of meetings in a wooded area out in nature. That sounded different to me, but exciting. We had befriended these folks and decided we needed to support them. Tom went one night with one of our church members. That night "Sister Geraldine" preached.

Mildred, one of the ladies of our church, asked me to attend with her. Her husband drove us there. He had gone the night before and said that he thought we would "enjoy" it. We entered a dark wooded area. We walked until we arrived at a well-lighted place. Logs were arranged for sitting. Several people were already seated. Mildred and I sat near the back. Her husband decided to lean against a tree in the back in a dark area. He was at the service, but not in the service.

It was a hot summer night, but not as hot as the preacher's sermon. He preached for a long time about hell with lots of brimstone. When he finished he had an altar call. Several kneeled to prayer at the altar. The preacher then said: "Will the lady sitting on the second row from the back, the second seat from the end come to the altar?" I looked around and realized that it was me. I got up not knowing why I was called out. He asked me to kneel that he felt that he needed to pray for me. When he finished praying, I got up and walked back to my seat. Then he asked Mildred to come forward.

On our way home, Mildred asked her husband why he stayed in the back. He said, "I knew what the preacher was going to do during the invitation, and I just wanted to see your reactions." He then said that the other night he attended, "a woman got the "holy ghost," jumped a bicycle and ran into the woods." I don't think that he came to the meeting that night for the right reason.

In a small community nothing goes unknown. The next Sunday, several commented about "our adventure." Miss Ethel, a neighbor and elderly church member approached me and said "didn't that disturb you that he would call you out like that"? I said "no not really, I feel that I can use all of the prayers I can get." More and more, as the years have gone by, I covet all the prayers that are said on my behalf.

Chapter 5

The Tornadoes

In 1974 we were still in the same church outside of Brandenburg, Kentucky. Tom was working on his doctorate and driving a school bus to make some extra money. His route went through downtown Brandenburg. After school, he would let the children off and immediately drive the bus home. It took him about thirty minutes to arrive home.

We will never forget April 3, 1974. Tom had just gotten home. We were standing outside looking at the sky. Toward Brandenburg the sky had the strangest dark colors. Our neighbor came home from work. He ran from his car and yelled "a tornado has just hit Brandenburg." He worked at a dairy in the city limits. They saw the tornado coming and took cover. Most of the building in which he worked was destroyed. All of his fellow workers had taken off to their homes in dread of what they were going to find.

Tom and a church member immediately got in our car and took off to see how they could help. The phone lines were out. We could not call out and no one could call in. It was Wednesday. Everyone was hearing of the devastation but that was all that we knew. Our church met for regular prayer meeting and that is just what we did.

I did not hear from Tom all night. The next morning he returned, exhausted and weary. He had been in the morgue all might, ministering to the families of those who were killed or injured. He told of the people he had talked with during the night. He listened to families as they spoke of the terror of the day and their deceased loved ones.

The community was in shock and families devastated with grief. More than one tornado hit Brandenburg that day and you could see the heartbreak everywhere. At the time several were still unaccounted for. Injured people were sent to several hospitals from Ft. Knox to Louisville. Some were unable to speak and others had injuries that made it hard to make identifications. The outpouring of companies, churches and people from all over the country was something that I had not seen before. Semi-trailers full of food and clothing came daily. The Red Cross was wonderful. The military guarded the community making residents feel secure.

The next two weeks, Tom and I continued to minister to hurting victims. I volunteered to help the American Red Cross. A nurse, two men and I went out in the county looking for people.

We arrived at one farm house to assist. A puppy was tied by the porch. He was very quiet, just sitting there. The family told me that the puppy was tied to a post next to their barn when the tornado came. The barn was totally destroyed. The puppy was found two fields away, tied to the same post. The wind had put it back in the ground with the puppy still attached. The veterinarian said that he was in shock, from his journey in the air, but would be alright. I picked him up and held him for several minutes. He started wagging his tail and I knew he would be alright.

Our previous church was in Indiana. The news was constantly telling of the tornadoes. The phone service was still out. An elderly church member, whose son was a police helicopter pilot, asked her son to fly over our neighborhood to see if we had been affected. When phone service was restored, she called to say what she had done. That concern made us feel good and know that she as well as others cared about us and our ministry.

During that time, we heard over and over about miraculous survivals and weeks of not knowing where loved ones were.

Questions were asked, especially "Why"? Why were some spared and others taken? We could not answer those questions. We could only try to give comfort, hope and lead them to the One who had the answers.

The night of the tornadoes, a reporter came to the morgue. He quoted Tom on the front page of the Louisville paper. A week later, Tom received a letter from a man in Arizona. Tom did not know him. He was expressing his view of why this happened. He stated that Brandenburg had to be a bad place for God to target that town and that it was because of the wickedness of the people.

I am sure that there were some wickedness in Brandenburg, but not anymore than anywhere else. Matthew 5:45 says "He causes his sun to rise on the evil and good, and send rain on the righteous and unrighteous" (NIV). Bad things happen to all people, good and bad. The important thing is faith to know that God will give strength and comfort to help us go through those things and be a better person in spite of them. The good in people is shown when others help with compassion and love. When the tornadoes came, the people also came to help restore a community and its people.

Chapter 6

He Came Back

We stayed in that small church over two years. We had a wonderful ministry with the community and church members. We learned to love the people but knew it was time to leave. It was hard for us financially. The church paid a part-time salary. The church said they could not afford to increase his salary. I had a hard time finding a job. I was always told that I had "too much education and was overqualified," whatever that meant. I did find a Social Work job a few months before we felt that it was time to leave.

Twenty years after leaving the church, Tom was called back to the church to speak at homecoming and a week of revival meetings. After the meal on Sunday, a church member approached us while we were getting in our car. We did not recognize him. He introduced himself. He was a member of the church when we were there, but stopped coming to the church while we were there. He was eager to tell us the reason of his abrupt exit of the church. We had always wondered why he stopped coming, but no one seemed to know.

He asked if we remembered the business meeting in which Lee, the minister of music, asked the church to purchase a water faucet to be attach to the outside of the parsonage. I remembered the situation, but vaguely remember the conversation in the meeting. He remembered it very clearly. I had planted flowers around the parsonage for beautification. We were having a dry spell. This was not an expensive item, maybe $5.00 at the time. It was a purchase for the church and we certainly could not afford it. A woman got up and said, "no one asked her to plant the flowers and I think that it is a waste of money." That was not the first time she had spoken hurtfully to us or others in a business meeting. Lee got mad and said "I will buy that faucet myself." No one else said anything and the meeting was over.

That was the reason that he stopped coming to the church. He did not want to worship with people who were unkind and mean-spirited. He also had relatives in the church and he was upset with some of them about the incident. He stopped attending the church and did not go anywhere else. After several years, he worked through his feelings and now was an active member again. Now he was in the right fellowship once again with other church members and his Lord.

I have never been in or known of a church that did not have some member(s) who by actions or words hindered the kingdom of God. There may be many reasons that people hurt others and cause dissension in a church, but the main reason is a spiritual need and Satan's strong hold in their life. It is sad that some never go back to their church or go to another church, but just drop out forever. They let the words of another cloud their love and service for the Lord. They let Satan get in control of their life and thoughts.

Ephesians 6: 10–11 says "Finally, be strong in the Lord and in his mighty power. Put on the full armor of God so that you can stand against the devil's schemes" (NIV). We drove away that day being thankful that this man had let the Lord have control over his life and he was now in the church fellowship once again.

Chapter 7

The Loving Church

OUR NEXT CHURCH WAS located near Elizabethtown, Kentucky. I could continue in the same job because it was in the same area. I was also pleased because we did not have to go far for groceries; we were close to a hospital, doctors and many other stores that might be needed. The people in the church appeared to be very happy with few problems.

The church had many elderly people in the congregation. One in particular, an 85-year-old lady and her husband always made us feel welcomed in their home. Many times, she would call in the morning and say that she was getting ready to make the biscuits. We did not want to miss her breakfasts. We would get ready and out the door we went. Ms. Iona would be in the kitchen, mixing the biscuit batter. She placed the biscuits on an iron skillet. She then would get busy on the rest of the breakfast, as I helped her. She always had some kind of breakfast meat and eggs. Her husband would gather the eggs fresh from the barn. We eagerly waited as the biscuits finished browning. Ms. Iona, her husband, Tom and I would eat to our heart's content. We then topped breakfast off with a warm biscuit, flowing with a pat of butter and jam or molasses. When we finished there were few biscuits left.

After being in the church for two years, our son David was born. Christmas was less than a week away. David was eight months old and it was to be his first Christmas. On the Wednesday before Christmas, Tom went and got Ms. Iona. She and I were baking cookies for a mission group that were having their Christmas party that night. We baked most of the morning. David had an ear infection and was taking an antibiotic. Around noon I fixed us a sandwich to eat and take a break. David started vomiting and continued for an hour. Tom called his pediatrician. He was out for lunch, but his receptionist told us to bring him in at 2:00. Ms. Iona stayed at our house to complete the cookies. We took David to his doctor. The doctor came in and immediately told us to go to the second floor of the hospital, which was the pediatric ward. We were not to stop at the emergency room. We did just that. The doctor got there and started an IV in David's head. The doctor said that it scared him to see David in that shape and that David would have died if we had waited any longer to bring him in.

Tom stayed with David. I went home, boxed up the cookies and took Ms. Iona home. I put my things in a bag and headed back to the hospital. On the way back, it was getting dark and started snowing. The road was slippery. I stopped suddenly for a light and almost ran off of the road. I finally got to the hospital. David was crying loudly. He had pulled the IV out of this head. The nurses could not get it back in and were awaiting the doctor to come back to the hospital to insert the IV. The doctor finally got the IV in place. They had to restrain his arms and legs.

That started a very long hard week for us. David could not have any visitors. His immune system was very low. He was on a high bed. It took one of us most times standing over the bed to keep him from getting to the IV. Christmas was on Sunday, we had not had a break and both of us were worn out. Some church members brought us a tasty Christmas meal. My parents were coming up that afternoon to see us, but they were not allowed to go in to see David. The only other person that they allowed in to see David was his babysitter, Dorothy. She came to the hospital, sat with David, and we went home for a couple of hours to have Christmas with my parents. David got to come home after being in the hospital for a week and half. That incident made us appreciate our son and the life that God had given us.

Dorothy had been David's babysitter since he was three months old. It was obvious she loved him and he loved going to her home. He would just smile when he saw her at church or anywhere. She had raised two wonderful children and we felt privileged that she would keep him while I worked. She taught him to suck his thumb. Dorothy said that sucking a thumb meant a contented child and he became an avid thumb sucker. I was concerned we would never be able to break him from the habit.

The summer after we left that church, David was three and still sucking his thumb. We had a week long summer trip planned with the youth in our new church. We kept in contact with Dorothy. In one conversation, she asked us to leave David with her while we went on the trip. We did and when we got back, he had completely stopped sucking his thumb. I don't know how she managed that miracle, but she did.

In the church, David was the only child of a staff member. He received special attention from the church members. Our neighbors, Claudie and Essie were also wonderful to us. They loved to play with David. Since our parents were not near they became substitute grandparents to David. The nursery at church was full of children, several were David's age. David never lacked friends and someone to play with.

One of the biggest revivals that we have ever experienced was in the church. We had a lay witness mission on a weekend. On Sunday, before the sermon, Tom gave an invitation. Several received Christ as their savior. Tom preached and gave another invitation. Again it was the same response. The next week he baptized until he was tired, but with a grateful heart. It was an exciting time.

Tom also was told that he could not complete his doctorate in his last church. After many meetings at the seminary, it was agreed that he could do his project in this church. After five long years of work, his project was completed. He wrote his thesis. Our friend, Marvin, his wife and young daughter came to our home. The children were put to bed. We sat around the kitchen table and passed the pages of thesis to each other one by one to check for errors. By morning we had all read the complete 176 pages. It was an exhausting night, but the thesis was ready to be sent to the typist. Thank goodness for friends who came to help us in our time of need! The church had not had a pastor to receive a doctorate. They had a party for Tom and gave him a beautiful navy blue suit.

It did not take us very long being in the church to realize that there were some personal and spiritual problems. There were dissensions and some people were not happy with their lives. Some were always looking for solutions other than the Lord.

However, I will have to say that the church was wonderful to us and they were one of the most loving congregations that we have had the privilege to be a part in ministry. With all of that love it was hard to leave, but it was time to go.

Chapter 8

Staff Friends In The Ministry

WE WERE NOT PLANNING on leaving our last church, but were called to another church, this time in Western Kentucky. It was hard move for us because of friendships made and especially because David had so many people who loved him. The unknown is sometimes scary and fear that you want have as loving or close friends.

In our first few weeks in the church we immediately became close friends with Gary and Sue. They had been in the church for about a year. We had not been in churches that had other full time staff. Gary had been called to be the Minister of Music and Youth. For several years we attended the youth camps with them. That was when I learned an appreciation for youth and their leaders. Partly, that was due to watching Gary and Sue and the wonderful work that they did. We also had a great working relationship with them and a personal friendship. We ate many meals at each other's homes.

I was a substitute teacher in the school system during that time. I worked with several of the teachers who attended our church. During our breaks, we talked of the problems facing teachers and the children. It gave me an insight into these problems. Since David was small, I was not aware of the situations that he would soon have to face.

When I was not working, David and I would take my three-wheel bicycle out for exercise. We had a 7-mile route. I pumped away at the pedals and David rode in the basket in the back. It was good exercise and gave use some bonding time. Also, it would give us time to visit with some elderly on our way there and back. At last was the grocery stop. David would hold the grocery bag in his lap on the way home.

While we were there I became pregnant. A month before delivery, I broke a rib and was put on bed rest. Both of our children were born in April. The week before Debra was born, David had his seventh birthday. With help from church members, I was able to give him a birthday party. We had a clown ministry in the church. One of the clowns showed up for the party. All of his Sunday school class showed up. I would not have been able to have the party if it had not been for all the church members' help.

Then Debra was born. From the time she was born, she never slept. Her first shots caused a reaction. She had colic and then ear infections. She constantly ran a fever. She was a sweet child, but day and night it was constant care because she cried a lot. It was hard on use to see her in so much pain. I am sure that I rocked a thousand miles in the rocking chair during that time. That was the only way that seemed to ease her. We took her to several doctors but none could give us answers about her ear problems. Tom and I had to take shifts at nights because she was up most of the night crying.

One of our church members was showing signs of strange behavior. People in the church talked about the things that she was doing. She would talk loudly in church services. Her conversation was not coherent. One day she left home, got lost and was found miles away. She had run out of gas. She did not know where she was and just started walking. The police found her, but she did not know her own name. At that time they did not know what she had. It was Alzheimer's disease. It did not have a name at that time, but it was my first time to see the effects of this disease on a person and their family.

The church needed a new social hall and space for Sunday school rooms. The church voted and decided to build. The church members worked on Saturdays to complete the addition. The men would work and the woman cooked lunch. I looked forward to Saturday because we had such a good time together. Most of the church was built by the members. When we got into the new building, it was paid for. The rooms filled up with classes so fast that it was discovered that more room was needed. The new facilities were a beautiful addition to the existing building.

Gary and Sue had their first child, Sarah. Our children played together and we were very pleased with the close bond we shared. But we sensed it was getting time for us to leave. A pulpit committee called and wanted to meet us. I jokingly told Sue that if the prospective town had a Wal-Mart store then I would know that it was God's will for us to take the church. I bought all of Debra's diapers at Wal-Mart. When we met with the pulpit committee, one of the first things mentioned was that the town had just gotten a Wal-Mart. Later, when we got home from the meeting I called Sue and we had a laugh. Of course, that is not why we went, but it was funny.

The day that Tom gave his resignation to the church, I cried like a baby. We felt that it was time to go, but hated to leave our friends in the church and especially Gary and Sue. With much anticipation we left not knowing if we would ever have close friends on a church staff again.

It did not take very long in our new church to find other church staff members that we would become close to and felt as if we were a part of their families We will never forget Lorene and Brenda and how their love made us feel welcome. God has always provided other church staff that we have had close bonds with. Those we could share our hurts, concerns, joys and praises. On the journey of ministry God always provides who we need in the form of flesh.

Chapter 9

Things Are Not Always What They Seem

WE WERE IMPRESSED THAT the pulpit committee drove a long distance to visit with us. Also, our visit on the church field for a trial weekend went very well. The church spoke of a need for an addition onto the church. They also stated that they wanted a pastor who preached, visited the hospitals and in the homes. These were attributes in which Tom was strong. He also had been through two building programs in other churches and Tom knew about building projects. It appeared that this would be a good match.

The move was six hours from where we had lived. It was winter and the weather was cold. Debra was eight months old and due to her ear problems did not travel well. She cried or fussed most of the trip. We did not think that we would ever get to our destination. Finally, we arrived to a beautiful, spacious house that would be our home.

Within the first year, the area started losing jobs and some church members left to other locations where they found jobs. It became obvious that some of the church did not want to add an addition to the church facilities as was once thought. Also some wanted a pastor who ministered and others wanted an evangelist.

I don't think that the committee really knew there was as much dissension in the church as to what people wanted.

We were on the church field less than a year when problems and misunderstandings began to arise. One problem seemed to be solved and another would surface. The church was a large church with several missions. We tried to focus on the missions and the great needs that were present. I had been in church with dissensions before but this became overwhelming. I did not know who to trust and was afraid to say much to anyone. I did have friends in which to confide, but I could not get a handle on what was happening.

During our second year in the church, Tom and David went fishing at a local dam. Tom did not see a trail and he and David started walking down large rocks near the dam. One of the large rocks shifted and Tom fell twenty feet on his back. He landed almost in the deep water. Tom could not move and David went for help. He was hospitalized twice. His first time in the hospital was for broken ribs and bruising of his vital organs, the second time two weeks later for pneumonia. His doctor told him that his belt saved him from being paralyzed. Not until years later did I realize the significance of the protection and grace of God.

As time passed by, there were always problems in the church. Some unhappy church members established a "secret" bank account. The stipulation was that the money was to be put in the regular church account only if we left the church by December of that year. If we were still there, then the money was to go for the Christmas mission offering. This was not an account that was approved by the church, just opened by a few church members. This group also met weekly on Thursday nights to pray us out of the church. They met at a church member's house across the street from the parsonage. They did not seem to care who knew what they were doing and some were arrogant about their actions. During a business meeting, the church voted to dissolve the account.

To this day, I do not like business meetings. I had never seen people behave as badly as some did during some of those meetings. Several times it was brought up to fire Tom. One particular meeting it came up again. An elderly lady spoke in favor of Tom. One of the men stood up and told her to shut up and sit down. She was visibly shaken. Why did we stay? It was simple: we continued to feel that God wanted us there. Also, we felt that you stay somewhere until God moves you. Running away from a bad situation did not seem biblical if you were placed there for a reason.

Through the years, Tom had sent out resumes, but nothing materialized. After almost ten years, it appeared that it was time to go. So much had happened, maybe too much. We did not feel that we could continue with all the problems and increasing dissension. It had taken its toll on us. The deacons asked for Tom's resignation and he gave it to them. We did not have another church in which to go. We were tired and hurt. A few years before, termination was something that happened only when the minister wasn't doing his job or had committed an immoral act. That was not the case. Tom worked hard. He hesitated to take a vacation due to the work load and never knowing what was going to happen. We asked for deliverance from the problems. We wanted the problems to be solved or the Lord to lead us to another church. The deliverance came, but not in the way that we wanted.

There were many loving, caring people in the church. Not only were we hurt, but the church was also hurting. The church secretaries were very supportive and upset about the situation. Some of the deacons wanted to help, but felt that termination was the best for us and the church. Many, we have kept in contact with through the years. The church gave us six months' severance pay. It was January. We could stay in the parsonage until August.

Our state and local missions were involved in an educational ministry to Russia. The church was to pay Tom's way. Friends, Gene and Suzanne were generous and paid for Tom's trip. This enabled him to go for two weeks and teach classes to Russian ministers.

This was a very difficult time for our family. As the time drew near that we were to be out of the parsonage, we were talking to a church. I did not want to move my family twice in a short time, so we waited until we knew for sure about the church. The church did not work out. Also, it was hard to find a place to temporarily move that we could afford. We looked at a few places to rent, but most were too expensive or too small and there were not many places to rent that were available in the area. I felt that some of the church members thought we were not going to move unless they gave us no choice. That was not the case and some wanted us out of town.

At the last minute, a friend and church member, Susan, found us a house to rent. The family did not want to rent it, but decided to rent it to us. We had already made arrangements for David to live with and complete his senior year in high school in case we moved. Now we did not have to worry about that. I continued in my job. Tom's family wanted us to move in with them in Florida, which was a nice gesture. We couldn't see uprooting our family to go all the way to Florida, not knowing what the future was to hold and what God wanted us to do.

Susan would come over every night and help me pack. She organized everything. If it had not been for her, we would never have gotten moved. I was unable to make any decisions even about packing. I worked as a Social Worker. At work I was fine. I was efficient and worked as well as I always did. When I came home, I couldn't function, I would fall apart. My chest hurt. I knew that I did not have a heart problem, but my heart felt like it was going to break. I cried a lot. I remembered some of the unkind things that were said to me and about Tom.

When people in the town found out that Tom had resigned, several people wanted my job. After all, there were not many state Social Work positions available. The people that I worked with never told me, until I was getting ready to leave my job that they had gotten calls and others coming in the office wanting to apply for my position. They keep me from that hurt. One of the hardest things for me was to meet church members in public and be ignored. I would speak. Some would and some would not acknowledge my presence. We lived in a small town and I was always seeing someone from the church.

During that time, God sent some wonderful people our way. The associational missionary was great. He visited and kept in constant contact with us. The people I worked with were wonderful. I never spoke to them about the church or problems, but they were always there for me. Many of them were not professed Christians, but by their actions no one would have known. We were to stay in the area for a while. We made our home on Doty Creek.

Chapter 10

Life On Doty Creek

It was August when we moved to Doty Creek in 1995. Doty Creek was the name of the hollow in which we were to live. The house that we rented was a beautiful four bedroom three-bath house. It was spacious with a den, kitchen, dining room and large living room. There was a creek running in front of the house and large trees in the front yard. In back of the house were rocks extending to the top of a mountain. In spite of our situation, we were provided with a beautiful place to stay away from the troubles that we had experienced. We were still close enough for David to drive to school and me to drive to work, but a pleasant getaway to come home to.

Tom was asked to be the interim pastor of a small church in a neighboring county. We moved our membership to a Baptist church at the mouth of the hollow. That was where Debra and I attended church. When it was nice weather, Debra and I would walk to church. The main problem with walking anywhere near was that the area had poisonous snakes. Rattlesnakes and copperheads were commonly seen. On Sunday night we had walked almost to the church when Debra stepped over a snake. It was alive, but did not bite at her. One of the neighbors heard Debra scream, he came out and looked at the snake. He said that it was a copperhead and that it looked like someone had run over it. He thought that it was probably stunned. He took it and finished killing it. Maybe God let a car drive over it to keep from biting Debra. I know I was thankful.

The people in that small congregation made us feel at home. They were friendly and loving toward us. It was a time for me to sit back with no responsibilities in church. At that time I did not need to teach or do anything but worship and have fellowship with other Christians. The children and leaders opened their hearts to make Debra feel at home.

During that time, so many thoughts and questions flooded my mind. Did God want us to stay in the ministry? Did He want us to go into denominational work? Maybe we needed to go into secular work and find a place in a church as members. Bi-vocational work might be the answer.

We had only one full time income and financially we started having problems. We had three vehicles. In a year's time we replaced two motors and four alternators. Only one alternator had a warranty. If anything was going to go wrong financially, it seemed that it did. Even the small things got irritating.

David did not get to play football during his last year in high school because he missed the bus for football camp. We moved on Saturday. The football team left the next day on Sunday morning. On Saturday they changed the time to leave and had no way to contact us since we were in the process of moving. I took him to meet the bus and they had already left. We contacted one of the wives of a coach. We were told that we could bring David to the camp. It was out of state and David, being discouraged, said that he did not want to go. It was a hard year for him in school. At the end of his senior year, David started having problems with his left shoulder. He had to have shoulder surgery due to a stress injury. Not only did David have the pain of our situation, but he had the physical pain from his shoulder. The thing that hurt us most was watching our children and knowing the pain that they were going through and not being able to do anything. Debra was younger and it did not affect her as much as David.

One day I was having a piety party, asking God over and over, why? I had always thought that God would protect us from this. We were committed to His service and to the church. I was taught not to give up and that God would always bring a Christian through. At that time I could not see the "big picture."

During that time, Tom and I went to a meeting for ministers and their wives who had gone through similar situations. That was the first time that I had heard other's express their hurts, needs and feelings of despair. It was a time of expression and understanding of shared feelings. We shared something special with the other ministers and their wives. I have wondered many times where they are today.

At home I would spend many hours in the living room. I would sit in a recliner and look out a big picture window watching the goats on a distant mountain side. They would run back and forth up the mountain as they ate the grass. They jumped and acted as if they did not have a care in the world. I watched as the seasons began to change. The leaves changed into beautiful colors and fell off the trees leaving them bear. The mountain became drab with no color until the snows fell and left a blanket of beautiful white on the ground. Then the trees budded again and flowers sprang up making the mountainside green again. In front of the picture window was where I read my Bible, prayed and listened to the Lord speaking to me. God used the goats and his seasons to help me understand His truths. The goats appeared to have faith that they were going to be cared for. My faith was being challenged to see if I had the faith to believe that God was going to take care of us. The changing seasons helped me to see that even through my family was going through a rough time of bleakness that the flowers were going to bloom again and God would bring us through.

On a spring day in late April, 1996, as the flowers were starting to bloom, we got a call to a full time ministry. We had been in that area for over eleven years. A big part of our life was there and now it was time to leave. We started packing our things to go to another part of the state. God had heard our prayers and he was not through with us. Those days were some of the most important times we spent. For me, it was by the big picture window watching the goats, reading, praying and listening. Tom and I had a better understanding of deep hurt of ministers and church members. We knew that the church was still God's way of reaching people and we were still a part of His plan.

Chapter 11

Lessons From Job

We moved to our new church field. Things in our new church were going good. A church family started having a Friday night prayer meeting in their home. I usually attended. During our prayer time a situation stayed on my mind. I remembered one person in our previous church that had tried different things over several years to get us out of the church, He wasn't the only one, but what made it bad was that we thought that he was a friend. At one time, Alan and his wife, Mary, would have us at their home regularly. It was nice to visit with them. We found out that loyalties sometime cloud peoples' thinking and their actions. When we found out some of the things he had done and said, we were very hurt. I felt that all I could do to help Tom was to pray and defend him if necessary. I was objective about criticism, but so much was not constructive, but hurtful.

David was in high school. He was having problems with all that was going on in the church. Alan had retired from his job and was substituting in the high school. I became concerned that because he disliked us that he would treat David unfairly. I wanted David to behave, but not treated unjustly. The more that I thought of the situation, the madder I got and concern for David. At that time, we did not need any more problems. The business meeting the previous month had been bad, with all kinds of unfound accusations. My motherly instincts took over. I did not know if he would try to cause a problem for David, but I became fearful. Then anger overwhelmed me.

The situation that stayed on my mind was a confrontation that I had with Alan. On a Sunday morning I was taking the enrollment book for Sunday School to the church office. As I went down the hall I came in contact with him. In the church hallway, I let him have it. I don't remember all that I said. When I get mad it is bad. My blood pressure was probably "out the roof." I told him not to bother our children. He said "Is that a threat?" I said "no." In church there was not much that I could do, but I could go to the principal or the board of education if necessary. I was prepared to do that if needed to protect David.

During one of the Friday night prayer meetings, I became convicted about my feelings toward Alan and that my actions were just as bad as his. Yes, I had a right to be angry for all that had happened, but I was not acting as a Christian in my response to him. I let the anger take control of me. James 1:20 says "for man's anger does not bring about the righteous life that God desires" (NIV).

I had been reading the book of Job. I came to the last of the book. In chapter 42 it said that Job prayed for his friends. Job's friends never helped him but used words of discouragement. Then I read verse 12: "The Lord blessed the latter part of Job's life more that the first" (NIV). That was the message that I needed and wanted for my life. I did not want to have wealth as much as blessings so that I could live more and more for God. God's blessings come in many ways. If a person desires to follow God just for the wealth, then they have the wrong motive.

God cleansed my heart that day and truly made me whole. I asked for forgiveness of my extreme anger. Don't get me wrong, we at times have a right to be angry but what we do with that anger is the important thing. Jesus said to be angry and sin not. Well, I got angry and did sin because I let it fester and grow. Through that cleansing, I have never been the same. I started praying for those who wronged me and forgiveness when I had done things that had not represented my Christian faith.

Years later, I asked David what kind of teacher Alan was. I knew that David had him as a teacher several times. David said that he was nice to him and that David liked him. I want to think that he would have been nice to David anyway. I will never know for sure. Ever since that time, I have prayed for Alan and Mary and asked that the Lord would bless their lives. Years later, God gave me the opportunity to receive a letter from Alan and respond back to him. I was thankful and felt that some bridges had been mended.

Job has become one of my favorite books of the Bible. There are many lessons to be learned from Job's life. Forgiveness is cleansing for the soul and an action commanded by Jesus. Job forgave his friends. I was learning to forgive those in our past who had hurt us. We had endured a very difficult situation, and sometimes wondered if we would make it.

Enduring is vital in the Christian life. Job endured through all that happened. He did not understand everything that was happening and why it was allowed, but he continued to endure. Job showed great faith that God was going to be with him and bring him through. Through faith, we had to learn to depend on the Lord like we never had before. Without faith, life would be unbearable.

In Matthew 17:20 Jesus was speaking to his disciples. He said "I tell you the truth, If you have faith as small as a mustard seed, you can say to this mountain, move from here to there and it will move. Nothing will be impossible for you" (NIV). A mustard seed is very small. Our faith may start out small but grows as our faith is exercised. Job held on in spite of all that happened to him. No way would I ever compare our situation to Job's, but the same God who was with Job, was with us. Great was his reward for his faithfulness and great will be our reward when we exercise forgiveness, endurance and faith.

Chapter 12

Pride

THE SAME CHURCH HAD need for a new sanctuary, social hall and offices. Again, that was one of the reasons that the church was interested in Tom, since he had experience in church building projects. He was ready for the challenge. Most of the church members were eager to get started with the building. There were a few still not convinced that the church needed to build. Tom spent time with them talking about their concerns and the church's needs. Most of the people got on board with the building fever.

Everything went fairly smooth during the building process. There are always some problems with a building project, but nothing major. The building was completed. The committee worked hard to make sure that the furnishings for the foyer and sanctuary made a beautiful place for worship. Those who came for weddings and other events stated that it was one of the prettiest sanctuaries that they had seen. Outside between buildings there was a prayer garden. In the foyer, Lori, a very talented church member, painted a mural depicting the life of the church. The uniqueness of the mural was that she painted church members in the scenes. Also, some of those deceased church members were painted in the mural as a tribute to their commitment to their Lord and church.

The sanctuary was built with the future in mind. It was spacious, for growth and expansion of membership. The church also had a need for change in music to meet the needs of all the members. The acceptance of blended music took a while and it was welcomed by most. The church members saw that all people's needs were being met in worship music.

I continued to meet with the small group on Friday nights for prayer. One prayer that I regularly prayed was for our sanctuary to be filled with people. We had a beautiful new sanctuary with massive space for growth. Others also prayed that same prayer. As time went by, I realized that one day that prayer would be answered, but that we might not be there to see the answer. We had been in the church for seven years and had seen a lot of needed change.

Pride got in my way. For weeks I protested to the Lord. All the work that Tom and I had done and why would God not let us see the results. Through prayer and study I was reminded of something that I knew but did not want to accept in this situation. God's ministers have different talents. He calls each for special assignments in his churches. Some may be called to build and some may be called to fill. In some situations that may be the same minister. Each minister is called to meet certain needs of the church at specific times. Also, a church does not belong to its members or to the minister, but it belongs to God. Galatians 6: 4 says "Each one should test his own actions. Then he can take pride in himself, without comparing himself to somebody else, for each one should carry his own load" (NIV). We had been there to complete the beautiful building and assist in needed changes.

After much prayer, discussion and sole searching, Tom and I accepted that our time in that church was drawing near an end. We had gone to the church for the right reason and we would be leaving for the right reason. Shortly, we received a call from a minister of music that we had previously ministered with saying that his church was looking for a minister. Tom had been on his mind as being the man that the church needed to lead it to get back on track. The church had problems but that did not distract us. We met with the pulpit committee several times, went to the church for a weekend trial service. The vote came and it was good. We prayed that God would make His will know to us. After much soul searching we decided to go to the church.

Chapter 13

God's Will

THE PULPIT COMMITTEE AND church had been honest with us about some problems in the church. We were impressed with their honesty. We had gone to churches having no idea what we were getting into until we got there. I am not saying that committees or churches lie to prospective ministers, but sometimes members are not aware of problems.

Some difficulties that the church had experienced caused the church to be depressed for the last several years. The church building was an old building that needed repairs. It appeared that not much had been done to the facilities for a long time.

The town we moved to was about an hour's drive from my job. It was a small town and not much prospect for me getting a job in my educational field. It meant that I would travel longer to get to work on winding country roads. I still had to work. I decided to make the best of the drive. I would sing, listen to Christian music, praise the Lord and pray.

The people in the church and community were nice to us. It did not take long to realize there was a lot of work to be done, especially with relationships in the church. Our first year, Tom focused on the fellowship of the church. We had regular meals and socials. It took a year, but the church members started to show that they liked being with each other and enjoyed the fellowship. I heard of times in the past of great revivals, love and fellowship. This was a renewal of some days gone by.

The church has many committed people from all walks of life. The church started growing with new members and ideas. New blood sparked new life and excitement. The church did not exclude anyone; all were welcomed. Tom and the Minister of Music led the church to install a video system that made worship more versatile. Although the idea was novel for this church and very costly, there was neither dissension nor division. Indeed, it took less than a year to pay the debt. It took a while to get accustomed to it but most enjoyed a new kind of worship. Now it would be hard to think of morning worship without it.

Then repairs began on the church facilities. Most of the work was done by church members. The facilities looked cleaner and pretty. The most important thing was that people were taking pride in their church and realizing that the house of God was a place in which members needed to be proud. Tompkinsville First Baptist was our home until January 2015, when Tom retired from the full time ministry. We were there for 12 years. I never thought that we would stay that long, but God had other plans for us. I felt blessed that He sent us to Tompkinsville to worship, share, love, and be loved with some of the greatest Christians that I have ever met. Tom's age, experience and wisdom helped the church and they were to us what we needed at this stage in our lives. It was the best church he could have retired from the full-time ministry and God knew that.

Before retiring, Tom took a class in being a transitional pastor. He has the desire to help churches when they need someone to fill in for them when their pastor is away. But his main desire is to help churches transition from one pastor to another, especially mentoring young ministers. Since retirement he has helped two churches as a transitional pastor. His reward has been seeing the churches have a smooth transition and seeing young ministers grow in Christ. He is also teaching an Old Testament class at our church. I have been teaching in women's ministries and speaking at retreats. We are excited about the future and where God will lead us to minister for Him. A minister or Christian may retire from their full-time pastorate or job, but should not retire from doing God's work.

PART II

Experiences And Lessons Of Life

Chapter 14

Not A Chance

IN OUR JOURNEY IN the ministry, there have been numerous situations that we have encountered. Some situations we have encountered more than once and others are onetime events. Some experiences have had everlasting effects on our lives and others we would just like to forget. One of the repeats in our ministry left us wondering why some people are so rude and where was their loyalty.

Early in our ministry we had just moved on the church field. On Saturday the church youth were playing softball in an associational league. This was the Saturday before our first Sunday at the church. We had only met the church members when we were there for the trial weekend. We thought that would be a way to meet the youth, their parents, and socialize with other church members.

As we were walking toward the baseball field we were first approached by a lady, a church member. Her two oldest children were playing ball. She just wanted Tom to know that she loved the last pastor and was upset that he left. She said that the last pastor was wonderful and that she was not going to like Tom or give him a chance. It gives a pastor a challenge when just meeting someone and knowing that you are not going to be given a chance to prove yourself.

She was true to her word. Critical of everything Tom did, she never had a nice or pleasant thing to say to either Tom or myself. We both tried to have a friendship with her, but to no avail. We did have a friendship with her children. We were in the church for over two years. The day that we moved, her husband came to the church parsonage. He said that he did not want us to get away before he apologized for the way his wife had behaved. He did not feel the same way and felt bad for her behavior. "If you think she's made your life hell, you ought to have to live with her. I'm going to leave her as soon as the kids are grown!"

Years later in another church, a similar situation occurred. Our first week in the church a member came to the parsonage, sat on the couch, and told me of her great love for the last pastor. She felt that no one could take his place. One time I thought that she was warming up to us, but pulled back. We had no intention of taking the place of her past pastor, but just wanted to be a friend and minister to her when needed.

Since that time, we have not met anyone else who was so verbal about their feelings. Some may feel that way but have not expressed it. We have had numerous close friends in the ministry, but most have accepted the fact that we left and did not cause a major problem for the minister that followed us. It has happened, but as we have matured in our faith, we have tried to help others understand that ministers come and go and that our ultimate loyalty should only be to God. After all, he does the calling and sending.

Most of the time when a minister leaves it is for a good reason. When a close connection between minister and church member occurs it is hard to let go. Ministers and their families do the same thing. When there is a problem and the minister is involved, sides are drawn and feeling hurt. Sometimes people leave the church because of a situation in the church with a beloved staff member. It is the responsibility of the minister who has left to encourage the member to try to stay and work out the problems if possible and as best not be a part of the problem. Also, to work toward trying to have a relationship with the new minister.

This may be idealistic, but it can work if the minister and church member realize that friendships will continue to last and that all in ministry serve the church not for themselves but for God. It is important that the new minister be given a chance for his ministry. It is healthy for the minister, individual and the church.

Chapter 15

The Ends Do Not Justify The Means

2 Timothy 2:24 says "And the Lord's servant must not quarrel; instead, he must be kind to everyone, able to teach, not resentful" (NIV). Ephesians 4:32 "Be kind and compassionate to one another, forgiving each other just as in Christ God forgave you" (NIV). 1Thess. 5:15 "Make sure that nobody pays back wrong for wrong, but always try to be kind to each other and to everyone else" (NIV). All of these scriptures speak of how we are to treat each other. It has always seemed strange to me, that some of the most hateful and hurtful words have been spoken in the church by "Christian people". It is alright to give an opinion, but to do it hurtfully is wrong.

I have sat through meetings and left embarrassed that people act and say terrible things about other church members. Supposedly, these are people with whom they will spend eternity. Not to mention the things said about staff members.

I have witnessed, in some business meetings, church moderators speak unkind words to some church members that do not share the same views. I have heard some of the most hateful crude comments come out of the mouth of church members. From conversation with other church staff, I have heard of others who have seen and heard similar things. The minister must guard himself from doing the same thing. I have seen ministers who have also wanted their way at all cost and hurt individuals with the idea they are right and that is all that matters.

When a person has strong feelings about a situation they need to express those feelings, but to attack others if they do not believe the same way is wrong. Is God's will my will? That is a question we should always seek to answer. Even if we feel that our will is God's, we must act with love in achieving that goal.

If the outcome is our desired goal, but we have deliberately hurt others by being mean and deceptive in the process, is that right in the eyes of God? I don't think so. Sometimes the fight is not worth the cost. All Christians need to learn, through prayer, to pick the right battles. All are not worthy. God is still in control. This goes for the church members and the ministerial staff. Some get caught up in also perceiving that they always know the will of God for the church in all situations.

Ministers get frustrated because they see so much potential in the church and things that the church should be doing. Sometimes it is a slow process to get people to see the same vision. That is when patience needs to be exercised. What might not work today, may work at a later time.

A church hired a new senior minister. It was felt that he probably would want his own ministerial staff. So they fired all of the existing ministerial staff. This was a large church. Some of the staff had been there for years. They were all left with nowhere to go. He brought in his own staff. He as well as his staff caused a lot of problems in the church. None fit in well with the church members. Within two years all were gone and the church left in a mess. What was wrong with the new senior minister learning to work with the existing ministers? What happened in this situation? Mistakes were made on the part of the church and the ministers and people got hurt. I know that in some situation there is no way to keep from people getting hurt, but we must always be aware of other's feelings.

Sometimes in a business meeting people show up to vote that haven't darkened the doors of the church for years. As long as a person is a member the by-laws says that they can vote, but is it right? If they haven't been there to know what is going on, how do they know how to vote? Usually this is because someone wants their way and they use inactive people to get their vote. To some, it does not matter what they do to get what they want.

We must never forget that the ends do not justify the means. Nowhere in the Bible does it tell us that is a biblical truth, just the opposite. Our action in the process tells about our character and our love of others. The world is watching the church and the minister and how they conduct business. Does our action reveal a loving and forgiving God?

Chapter 16

Provisions

WHEN I WAS A child in Sunday school I had a teacher who stated one Sunday that she prayed for everything. Mrs. Ausbrooks had five children. She told of her children needing clothes and shoes for school. She and her husband had trouble just buying the necessities. She said that she always prayed that the Lord would lead her to the right stores to purchase the items the children needed. Everytime that she prayed God would lead her where the sales were and that the Lord had always supplied for her family and their needs. That statement stayed in my mind and many times would come back to me especially when we did not have money when needed. I have prayed times when we had little money and God has led me to stores where there were sales and just what we needed.

God also uses individuals to help others in their need. When we have had a need, God's people have always been there. One of the churches that we were called to had planned on giving us a raise when we got on the church field. After being there for six months, the church decided that a raise was not something that the church could afford. Only Tom was working with a part-time salary. We received a telephone bill in the mail. It was for a little over $24.00. We had no idea where the money was coming from. We prayed about the situation. The next day I went to the mailbox. There was a letter. It was from a couple from a neighboring community. The letter said that they had heard of all the good things that were happening in the church and wanted to help us. A check for $25.00 fell out of the envelope. God used people that we did not know to help us.

I finally got a job after almost a year. The problem was that I did not have any clothes to wear to work. I had not bought anything since we could not afford it. I was going to start to work on Monday. My birthday was on Sunday. That Sunday night, the church had a surprise birthday party. I received five outfits of clothing, one for each working day of the week. Numerous other gifts were given to me, all that I could use. It was such a shock for me. Again, God use His people to supply my needs.

In the same church the minister of music worked full time at Ft. Knox. We lived twenty-two miles from a laundry mat and did not have a washer and dryer. One day Lee Parr drove up with a used washer and dryer. They were rebuilt appliances from Ft. Knox. He wouldn't take any money for them. It did not matter to me that they were used. Both continued to work for more than ten years. We really got our money out of those appliances.

We moved to our next church with little furniture. All that we possessed were odds and ends. The day we moved, a church member took me to the furniture store and had me pick out a leather living room set, complete with lamps and end tables. The church wanted to do something nice for us. We had it upholstered after ten years. Afterwards we keep the living room set from years. Later, when we could afford a new set, we gave it away to a family that was in need. It was hard to give it away, because of the love that had been put in that present. When I think about it today, I still think that was the prettiest living room set that I have ever seen.

Our children were born in different churches. The churches made sure that both children were taken care of. The showers that they gave us provided for their needs for at least a year. David was seven years old when Debra was born. I had the same due date for both children. David was born on April 10th and Debra the 15th of April. When they gave me a shower for Debra, they also gave David presents that made him feel special.

The year and half that we were out of a church was a hard financial time for us. God always sent others our way to help us. Some from the church we left. That Christmas the association made sure that our family had Christmas. They brought us a bountiful meal and money for the children's Christmas. They made that time special for us to know that we were provided for.

In another church after building a new sanctuary, the church was encouraging members to buy furniture for class rooms and offices. Charlie and Sue bought beautiful furniture for the pastor's study. Tom's office furnishings were some of the nicest in the building. When the new building was built, there was less grass to mow. Church members took turns mowing the lawn. Part of our agreement, when we came to that church, was that our lawn would be mowed. Some did not want to mow the parsonage lawn anymore since there was not much grass to mow at the church. There was much discussion about the parsonage lawn. A church member took Tom to a local store, had him pick out a large riding lawn mower and paid for it. It solved the problem and was a nice gesture and something that we still use.

There have been many times that God answered our prayers and met our needs. He usually provided for us with more than what we needed. Philippians 4:19 "And my God will meet all your needs according to his glorious riches in Christ Jesus" (NIV).

We have the desire to help others like we have been helped. If we listen to God's voice he will reveal to us the needs of others. God uses our words and deeds to accomplish His purposes, both are important. God has used others to provide for us through the years and out of our blessings we have the desire to help others and share as God has given to us.

Chapter 17

Talents

In March 1995, I came down with a virus and was sick for days. I got over the weakness and sick feeling, but my voice was raspy and could hardly speak. My doctor told me that I was not to speak for two weeks in hope that resting my vocal cords would solve the problem. After the two weeks I still could not speak louder than a whisper. He decided to send me to a nose, ear and throat specialist.

The weeks turned into months of seeing the specialist. He decided to take a biopsy of my vocal cords. He did not find anything. Then I realized that I had lost my singing voice. I had not been the best vocalist in the world, but I could sing and felt that I did have a talent. I enjoyed singing in the church choirs and solos. Now it seemed that the talent was gone. I grieved about the loss.

I was still having problems with my voice when we moved in 1996. I was sent to another specialist. He performed another test on my throat and vocal cords. He said that I had scar tissue on my right vocal cord. His diagnosis was that the biopsy caused the scar tissue. He did not give me much hope that my voice would come back. When I asked him about singing, he stated that I probably would not be able to sing again.

One Sunday in 1998, after much prayer I was able to sing a solo and join the choir. It was nice to sing in the choir again. Between allergies and scar tissue my singing is limited. But mostly from spring till fall my voice is clear. Since that time, I have taken every opportunity that I have to sing. Since my voice has deepened, I have learned to choose songs that are suitable for an alto.

Teaching is another talent that God has given to me. When we go into a new church I do not like to take another's place to teach. I feel that each should use their talents and it is not my place to take another's place teaching because I am the pastor's wife. But I have always had plenty of opportunities to teach.

I have done about everything in the church at one time or another and some things I have not been comfortable with. I did them because no one else would volunteer. I have come to the conclusion that the minister's wife does not need to take on too much. It loads her down and she does not enjoy working for the Lord. This is also the way that it is with some church members. They do everything and sometimes burn out. God does not want that because we can't enjoy God's people if we are stressed all the time. It is not the responsibility of one to do everything. It is a shared responsibility.

It is easy to take for granted the talents that God has given us. The old saying, "if you don't use it you will lose it" is true. If we lose our talent(s), then we wish we had them back. In the church, I have seen many people who have limited themselves. They never came up to their potential. They could do so much more for the church and the kingdom of God.

Sometimes we are afraid of what others will think or that we cannot do something as well as someone else. Some people with excellent talents never use them, fearing criticism. Others don't want to put out the effort to cultivate their talents. The Bible is full of people who were just available to do God's will. They did not always have great talents, but God used them and their talents became extraordinary tools of ministry.

Chapter 18

Marriage

We have seen all kinds of wedding ceremonies. Some weddings have been small with little family support. Others have been elaborate ceremonies that were very costly and an abundance of family present. Tom has officiated in ceremonies with the brides dressed in beautiful white gowns and one wearing a bright red dress. All have been unique in their own way.

The size or cost of the wedding may be important to society or the family but has little to do with the length of the marriage. Some marriages appear to be made in heaven, but last a short time. Others seem as if the marriage would not last a week and after years the couple still has a healthy, loving relationship.

In these years I have learned a lot about marriage from watching and talking to couples who have been married 50+ years. What I witnessed and learned growing up has been the most influential lessons in my life, my parents' marriage.

Daddy worked long hard hours, but provided for his family. He was committed to his family, but commitment to his Lord was above everything. This was reflected in the way he treated my mother, his family and friends. Mother had a strong commitment to the Lord, which was evident the way that she treated my father. She was supportive of my father, especially his activities at church.

Divorce was not in my parent's vocabulary. They were totally committed to each other. They did not always agree on everything but they never were contentious. When my father retired, they were able to take vacation together. Before my father got sick and died, they were blessed to have many sweet memories together. Mother took daddy home and cared for him until the day he died. They were not perfect people, but they were willing to work together to make their marriage work and their love for each other was obvious.

From my parent's marriage and all the marriages that I have known, it is apparent that marriage is a commitment. The marriages that work are those where the couple doesn't just live under the same roof, but there is a mutual love and respect. Just because a marriage starts off badly does not mean that it cannot survive and be a healthy marriage. It takes a lot of work, but it can become a viable union. If a marriage starts off great that does not mean that it will continue that way. If too much is taken for granted then it is only time before problems arise. If a couple think that their marriage has no problems they will soon find out otherwise.

In Genesis the Bible speaks of marriage and God creating man and woman. Hebrews chapter 13:4 says "Marriage should be honored by all" (NIV). Marriage was created by God. When biblical teachings are applied to marriage by husband and wife then marriage will work. After years of marriage, working through the problems, then a couple will know that God brought them together for a reason. By the grace of God and commitment, marriage will be all that it is supposed to be. Tom and I have experienced joy and laughter, tears and sadness, good and poor health, not enough money to pay bills and abundance, fear and faith. But through it all, God has given us the strength and courage to continue to love and respect each other and to work toward a biblical marriage.

Chapter 19

Parenthood

ONE OF THE HARDEST things that I have encountered in the ministry has been raising my children. Trying to teach them so that they would be well balanced was my goal. My biggest desire was that they learn to love the Lord. Being involved in church activities were important, but also to be exposed to school and community activities. The church also has expectations of the minister's family. Sometimes those expectations are not fair to the pastor's family.

For years, it was hard for me to take what some said as a "grain of salt." However, I learned to weigh what was said, pray about it and listen to the Lord for advice. Well-meaning people sometimes give poor advice about raising children, especially toward a minister's child. Minister's children are like everyone else's children. They act like children.

When our son, David was born, our church rallied around us. He was the only minister's kid that the church had had in a long time. They spoiled him. Whatever he wanted, he got. He was a sick baby into his second year. We did not have to ask, the church was always there to help. I knew that he was being cared for physically, emotionally and spiritually.

There are seven years between our children's ages. Debra was loved by all of our church members. She was sweet and cute. As a baby she was sick and running high fevers, which caused some learning disabilities. Her babysitters were always in the church. As an infant, she stayed at Debbie's home with other children from the church. When we moved, the church had a daycare. At that time I did not work, but Debra enjoyed the children so much that she asked to go daily to play with the others.

When David was in his teen years, things for us became difficult. Our church situation had many problems. David saw some of the worse behaviors of people that profess to be Christians. One lady, in our church, accused David of doing something that he did not do. When she found out the truth, she called me and apologized. I told her I appreciated the call, but she needed to apologize to David. She never did.

The neighbors that lived directly behind the parsonage were also church members. I talked with the woman about a situation in the church. She accused us of doing something that we did not do. She got mad and locked the gate between the houses. Our children used the gate most days to visit with other neighborhood children. No longer were they able to go through the gate. Neither one understood. I had to talk with them. I did not want them to have ill feelings toward her. That was hard when we were struggling with those feelings ourselves.

About the same time, Tom was dealing with a young man who had mental problems. His wife had left him and Tom had helped her get transportation to her sister's home. He got mad because Tom would not tell him his wife's location. He found out about our son, his name, where he went to school, when and where he got on and off of the school bus. The sheriff's office took out a restraining order on the man because of his threats toward Tom and David. We had to tell David about the situation. He never did hurt David, but it was a fearful time. The young man was put in jail for another offense and eventually left town.

Debra was too young to understand all that was going on during that difficult time in our lives. Meanwhile, David rebelled. For several years, he wandered away from the Lord. He did not want to be like the hypocrites that he saw in the church. Yet he knew that there were some very good Christians in the church who loved him. This was a difficult time for us. We worried about him, and feared what might happen until he could see his way back. I clung to Proverbs 22:6 "Train a child in the way that he should go, and when he is old he will not turn from it" (NIV). I had always said that David belonged to the Lord. But one day I finally gave him completely over to the Lord. I knew God had a plan for David's life, I just had to let him go. Letting God take control is the best thing we can do for our children.

Out of trade school and working, our son met some Christian young men. Together they started a Christian band. David's passion is playing the guitar. His playing provided an avenue for him to use his talent and serve God in the music ministry at his church. That started his healing. A few years later, David met Gretchen at church. She is one of the most wonderful Christian young ladies that I have met. I have the privilege of calling her my daughter-in-law. Together, they serve the Lord in their church. I am so proud of the Christian man he has become.

Debra lives with us. She works in the nursery ministry in our church. Debra goes on mission trips and always looks forward to the next one so that she can serve the Lord and help people. She loves acting and being a part of our community.

I have made mistakes in raising my children. I know that I have not always said the right things and showed the best responses to situations. At times my hurts have gotten in the way of being the Christian mother that I needed to be. In spite of my failures, God has been merciful and held my children in his hands.

Chapter 20

Gossip And Rumors

SOME OF THE WORSE things in the church are rumors and gossip. Christians sometimes don't participate in what they call "the big sins" but think that it is alright to spread gossip and rumors. I have heard people say "well it is the truth" meaning that it is alright to participate in spreading something about another.

Years ago, I remember a lady in my Sunday school class. After tests and counseling, her doctor discovered that she had a chemical imbalance. She needed to be hospitalized to get medications regulated. Her doctor admitted her to the rehabilitation section of the hospital. When hearing of the section of the hospital in which she was admitted, another lady in the church said "she must have an alcohol problem." That rumor spread like wildfire. When she came home and found out about the rumor, she was embarrassed and felt hurt that anyone she went to church with would say such a thing. It took several months before she went back to the church because of the gossip. The sad thing is that some never go back to church because of something said about them.

Proverbs 16:28 says "A perverse man stirs up dissension, and a gossip separates close friends" (NIV). Throughout our ministry, I have heard things about my husband and children and other staff members that were outright lies. I have always felt that I wanted to set the story straight, but have found that some people rather believe something false than to listen to the truth. A rumor is more exciting and some people are looking for excitement.

Some things said are the truth. Does that justify a Christian to continue to spread the gossip? The Bible says in Proverbs 11:13 "A gossip betrays a confidence, but a trustworthy man keeps a secret" (NIV). If the rumor is the truth, then the individual and their family will suffer from the situation. They don't need anyone's help to suffer for a sin. If no one else knows, God does. In the end, we always suffer for our sins. If we want to be trusted, then we need to be trustworthy. A person will not continue to share with those that they know will spread words that have been entrusted to them.

Some people do not realize the devastation of words until they are said about them. Then it becomes personal and they realize how others feel. When we learn to live by the golden rule, then we will understand others and our responsibility to them as fellow Christians. Matthew 7: 12, says "So in everything, do to others what you would have them do to you" (NIV).

Chapter 21

ONE SUNDAY MORNING WE were introduced to Kay at church. She professed to be a Christian. She was raised in church. For years, she was sexually abused in the basement of her home church. The images of her abuse stayed with her into her adult life. For years she had suffered mental illness, due to the horrors in her childhood.

She came to our church for the right reason; because she loved the Lord and wanted to worship with other Christians. After coming to our church for three years, Kay joined our fellowship. She was asked to leave another church. Sometimes she became loud and excitable. She was different and not like most of the ones who attended the church. However, she appeared to be treated well from the church members.

Tom and I visited in her home often. She would call for us to come to supper. When we got there, I would usually finish the meal. She was nervous and would sit down and talk, but she loved to" feed the preacher." We would talk for hours, sharing our faith. Our backgrounds were different, but we shared a common desire, to love God and serve others. She was eager to help and pray for those in need. She did anything that she could do at the church.

She and I attended a Bible study on Sunday nights. She always had a long list of people in need of prayer. She was eager to pray for them. She always wanted to know if she could do anything else to help.

Kay started spending long stays in the mental ward at the local hospital. She was in the hospital more than she was at home. One Sunday afternoon she called to say that she had just gotten home from the hospital. As soon as she felt better, she wanted to prepare supper for Tom and I. She also said that she missed being in church and was looking forward to getting back to worship services.

After church that night, her husband called to say that Kay had suddenly died of a heart attack. That night I couldn't sleep. I struggled with her death. I wondered if we as a church had done enough for her. I knew that each member, individually, would have to answer that question. She had told me, in one of our conversations, she felt loved and accepted in our church. For that, I was thankful.

After reading Matthew 25: 35–40, I was assured. Verse 40 says "And the King will answer and say to them," 'Assuredly, I say to you, inasmuch as you did it to one of the least of these my brethren, you did it to me' (NKJV). I felt grateful that God sent Kay to our church and into my life. Her prayer in life was to be healed. She had gotten an answer, a permanent healing.

Chapter 22

McAdoo

OUR FAMILY DOG, TYSON died. All the children in the neighborhood loved him. We had a funeral with all of the neighbor children attending. All of us were crying. A fellow Social Worker raised registered boxer puppies. One of her dogs had a liter and the mother had laid on one of the puppies legs. He had a slight limp. When she had found out about our dog dying, she asked me if we wanted the puppy. The veterinarian thought that his leg would be alright within time.

I went and looked at him and thought he was ugly. I had never been around a boxer dog. I told Tom and the children to go look at him and see if they wanted him as a pet. I stayed at home. After a couple of hours, the door suddenly swung opened and in ran the dog. I was sitting in the recliner. He ran, jumped in my lap as if to say "I am home." We registered him under the name of Tyson McAdoo Fire Maid Stokes. We used his father and mother's names as well as our beloved Tyson.

This was during the time that we did not have a church. McAdoo was with Tom during the days. They went for long walks and became close companions. He had the best personality. All he wanted was love and he would cock his head as if to say he understood exactly what we were saying to him. At home, wherever one of us went he would go.

He moved twice with us. Tom and Debra built him a dog house and I painted it canary yellow. It was big and stood out. Once he had heart worms. He was three years old. We had him treated and he got well. Two years later, he got sick again. We took him to the veterinarian. This time the doctor said that he had cancer. We could send him to be treated but the cost would be in the thousands of dollars. We could not afford that and there was no guarantee that it would help. We decided to care for him as long as we could.

Debra did not want us to put him to sleep. I told her that when he got to where he could not walk or was suffering too much, we would have to put him to sleep. He slept beside her bed at night. He had started having seizures. One morning, he walked over to Debra. He got as close as he could get to her, fell down and died. We were glad that we did not have to put him to sleep.

I was thankful that my friend, Vicky, was gracious enough to think of us when we lost our pet. I was thankful that during a difficult time in our lives that McAdoo took some of the pain. Some may think that what I am saying is silly but I believe that God can use all of His creatures to help, comfort and love. Genesis 1:25 says "God made the wild animals according to their kinds, the livestock according to their kinds, and all the creatures that move along the ground according to their kinds. And God saw that it was good" (NIV).

Chapter 23

Laughter In The Church

SINCE I WAS A child it did not take much to get me tickled especially in church. Some consider laughing in church to be irreverent. Since I married and started my journey as a minister's wife, many funny things have happened in the churches that we have ministered. But a situation that happened to me before I married gave me an insight into the fact that all churches are different. Some you fit into well and others you do not and sometimes you can't keep from laughing.

As I have mentioned before, my first job was as research assistance with the Sunday School Board (Lifeway) in Nashville, Tennessee. My friend, Lynn, and I were hired at the same time to do similar jobs. We were both single and enjoyed traveling. On weekends we would take off and visit friends. We always had a good time. It was just nice to get out of the city, enjoy the fresh air and look for new adventures. As we traveled we would sing. Lynn sang alto and I sang soprano.

Lynn had graduated from Howard-Payne College in Texas. The dean of students of the college had taken a new position at another college in North Carolina. One weekend we decided to go to North Carolina to visit with her. The mountains of North Carolina were beautiful. It was the fall of the year. We enjoyed our visit with Lynn's friend and my new made friend. We sat for long periods of time gazing at the multicolored leaves on the trees in the mountains. We got up early on Sunday mornings, sat on the porch looking at the mountains with all of their colors, and decided that we would take our time driving back to Nashville. As always, on our trips, we would pack clothes to attend church. We thought that we would be near Ashville, North Carolina at 11:00 and would attend First Baptist Church for morning worship.

This was 1970. The mini skirt was in fashion. Lynn and I decided to be stylish. She wore a bright red dress with black tights and I wore a blue dress with blue tights. My dress was a little above my knees and hers a little below her knees. Compared to the style of the day we were dressed conservatively. Setting off our attire we wore big shiny charm bracelets.

We misjudged our time and came through Ashville early. We decided to travel on and stop at the nearest exit close to 11:00 and find a church. As we traveled all we saw was country. Finally, at 10:50 we took an exit. We had no idea where we were. We passed two churches and finally saw a Baptist Church that said "affiliated with the Southern Baptist Convention." After all, we were Southern Baptist and worked for the Southern Baptist Board. The only place to park was directly in front of the church.

We were late, but went in and sat down on the next to the last pew. I looked around and noticed that all of the ladies were dressed more conservatively with hats and longer dresses. I began to think that our dress might be too much for these people.

During the offertory, the pastor came back to us and said "ladies, it is good to have you today. Will you provide special music for us?" He did not ask, but we told him our names. We went on to give him more information; that we lived in Nashville and worked at the Sunday School Board. After all, we were young, right out of college and proud of our jobs. Without blinking our eyes, we said "yes" we will sing. We conversed and decided to sing "In Times Like These". We sang that song a lot as we traveled.

The pastor introduced us. We started up the aisle jingling all the way. The congregation looked at us with stares. Of course, we had no music or anyone to play the piano for us. We started to sing. We forgot that on the second verse one of us would reverse the words and sing different words. When we got to the verse, the same thing happened. Then the usual happened, I got tickled. I did not want the congregation to think I was laughing, so I put in a few coughs. Lynn kept singing. She knew that I was tickled. She did not want them to think that I was laughing so she put her arm around my shoulder as if to console me. Well, that made things worse. Finally, I got composed enough to sing the last verse.

I could hardly wait until we got back to our pew and sat down. Actually, I wanted to crawl under the pew. The pastor said "let's pray." We bowed our heads and Lynn started laughing. She was usually the serious one. Well, that started me laughing again. The whole pew shook. I looked up and a woman was giving us an evil eye. We probably should have left them, but did not want to cause anymore commotion.

The preacher started preaching. His whole sermon was on the evils of living in the city, the awful dress of the young ladies and how Satan was using fancy sport cars to entice young people. He preached for a good forty-five minutes. It seemed like eternity.

The invitation was extended through two songs. We both felt that he was waiting for us to walk the aisle. When the invitation was finally over, Lynn said "let's get out of here before the preacher finishes the benediction." The only problem was that the preacher prayed and walked to the back door at the same time. He was at the door when he finished praying. We greeted him. He did not ask us to come back.

We walked to Lynn's car and got in. She backed up and turned her bright cherry red Mustang around in the front of the parking lot. It appeared that most of the church people stood there watching as we drove off. We got a few miles up the road, pulled over and become hysterical. Lynn and I felt that we had been in the wrong church and in the wrong pew. For months we laughed about that church visit.

We are to be reverent in church, but sometimes laughter is appropriate. I have come into contact with Christians who have a keen sense of humor. They laugh and are not afraid to express it. I have learned not to take myself too seriously and that laughter is good for the soul. Sometimes laughter comes from immaturity and sometimes things are just funny.

In the ministry, we see so much heartache and sadness. Sometimes laughter becomes a pleasant release. The book of Ecclesiastes chapter 3 talks about there being a time for everything. Ecclesiastes 3:4: "a time to weep and a time to laugh" (NIV). Laughter is a gift from God. He knows our heart and no one needs to judge our motive.

Chapter 24

Worship

THERE ARE MANY SONGS in our hymnals and praise songs that speak of worship. Most that I have heard talk about attributes of God and our response to him. Styles of worship differ in each church or denomination. Some worship with raised hands, shout, say amen, speak in tongues and wash others' feet. Some worshipers sit very quietly with eyes closed or raised toward heaven.

When I was in elementary school, I went with a neighbor to her small country church. The preacher was yelling his sermon. All of a sudden, the lady right behind me stood up and shouted. I had never heard anyone shout in church, especially in my ear. It scared me. I was afraid to move in fear that she might shout again or do something else. The service was one that I was not accustomed to attending and left me with the fear of going back to that church.

Some people are very critical of the way other people worship when it is different from the way that they worship. Sometimes it is because they are afraid that the Holy Spirit might get a hold of them and they might exhibit some behavior foreign to themselves. A question that some Christians often ask themselves is "What will others think if I get excited about my faith." Some attend worship and never show any emotion or response to words sung or spoken. Watching them, they appear that they are bored and act as if they receive nothing from the service. Reverence should always be shown in worship, but people have different ideas of reverence.

John 4:24 says "God is a spirit: and they that worship him must worship him in spirit and truth" (NIV). John 8:32 "And you shall know the truth, and the truth shall make you free" (NIV). When we are free in Christ we are responding to him without fear of what others will think or say. We focus on God and that is what he desires.

Worship and the method needs to be from a serious heart of love. When the Lord impresses on us to react to his love, we need to act in a way that pleases him and not others. After all worship should be between the individual and God.

I have heard criticism from those who never show emotion and those who show excitement about their worship. Each criticizing the other for not being spiritual enough or thinking that they have a "piece of God" that the other does not have. The main thing is that worship be an extension of life each day of the week. Not just at church, not for show, but from a sincere heart and expression of one's love for the Lord. Our friends, family, and co-workers will know if our worship on Sunday is real by the way we live our lives in front of them through the week.

Chapter 25

Living In The Parsonage

WE HAVE ALWAYS LIVED in a parsonage. The churches in which we have served have always provided a home for the minister and family. Some have been spacious with a beautiful interior and others have been small and in need of repairs.

Our first church was in a rural setting. The parsonage was an old house that needed repairs. The parsonage was next door to the church. There were numerous keys to the house. The biggest problem was that on Sunday morning a few church members would come in our home without knocking. I guess that since the church owned the house, some felt that they had the right to come and go as they please. It could also get embarrassing, since we were getting dressed for Sunday school and find someone in our living room.

The next house in which we lived was nicer. By that time our son David was born, the house was larger and more spacious. When Debra came along we had plenty of space and have ever since.

One of the problems we encountered has been that only necessities got fixed and sometimes they didn't get repaired. Time for remodeling was between ministers. Of course, when we moved we were the recipient of the new fixtures. While in the church the home provided, nice or not, still does not belong to the minister and family and is a temporary home.

The parsonage has and still serves a purpose. Especially when the church is located in a remote area and housing is hard to fine. Today, more churches are providing a housing allowance and using the parsonage for other things or selling it. Some churches will not consider giving a housing allowance since they already own the parsonage. They feel that is sufficient.

Ministers and their families deserve to have the same privilege that the church members have, that is to buy their own home. They need to learn how to manage with a house payment. The problem may be a down payment. Some churches work out ways to help the minister.

If the minister has always lived in a parsonage, upon retirement he has no home. The minister's income is not always enough that he can save for a house when he retires. Especially since the parsonage is part of his income package. Buying a house is a major concern for the retiring minister and may make it hard to have enough money to live. I know that the church has provided a house to help the minister, but in some ways it has hurt him for the future.

Chapter 26

Working Outside Of The Church

Since my children were born I have had two full-time jobs. While the children were small I worked part-time, mostly as a substitute teacher. We needed the extra money and I did not have to feel pressured if the children were sick. Debra was small. She enjoyed going to the daycare that our church operated and was always telling me she wanted to go play. At that time, due to the uncertain situation in our church, I felt that it was time for me to go back to work, mostly for my mental health. A Social Work position became available. I applied and got the job. That job was a lifesaver.

I loved the job. I stated working with prenatal woman and later worked with a Medicaid program in our County. A large percentage of the people that I worked with were elderly. I wanted to make sure that my job did not interfere with the church. I also was constantly examining my actions working in the secular world so they reflected my commitment to the Lord.

I made home visits. I was told when I first started that people could be clannish and to be careful where I went. Also, I was not from that area and might not be accepted.

I was cautious, but never had a problem. I tried to respect all of my clients and in return they respected me.

While in that position one of my co-workers was Gina. She had two miscarriages. The second time, she lost twins. We spent a lot of time talking about her loss. We shared scriptures for encouragement. A few years ago, she called. She had family that lived in the county in which we now live. She stops by to see me when she is in the area. Since that time, she has gone through a lot of hard times but still remains faithful. Our friendship has remained strong. Each time I see her I can see the love of God living in and giving her strength.

My last full-time job is the one in which I just retired. I was a program coordinator who provided services for the aging as well as working with people with disabilities for twenty-one years. I also supervised social workers. Each social worker has been special to me as I have seen their unique talents of working with the elderly/disabled as well as watching them grow in their abilities to help this most vulnerable population. My work has been an extension of my love for people. I have found ways to minister without be offensive and respecting others. I feel that God gave me my jobs and I have tried to listen to Him to know how I can be a help and comfort to others.

I have heard people say that the secular work place is a hard to work. I really don't believe that. Working in the church can be one of the most difficult and stressful places when you are dealing with peoples' problems. The most important thing is to respect and value people no matter who they are. They are still a child of God. I find that most of the time they will return that respect.

Whether we work in the church, in our home or in a secular job we need to do our best and give our all. Colossians 3:17 says "And whatever you do, whether in word or deed, do it all in the name of the Lord Jesus, giving thanks to God the Father through him" (NIV).

God always gives us what we need and I feel that he gave me the opportunity to work especially with the elderly. He has given me many grandparent figures in my work and in the church that have treated me like a granddaughter. The love of a grandparent that I missed as a child has been given to me as an adult. Isn't it amazing how God works?

Chapter 27

Ministers' And Wife's Conference

For several years, Tom and I have gone to a conference in January for ministers and their wives. This has been some of the best time that we have spent with each other. Also, we see many faces that we haven't seen since the year before. These conferences have become important to us. They are designed for our particular needs.

It is good to see familiar faces with similar problems. We spend hours visiting with others, talking about our families, problems, failures, successes and getting reacquainted. Some friends we have known for years, others we have just met and grown to love.

I have sat at the back of the conference watching the reactions of others while speakers were speaking and worship leaders were leading praise. Some speakers mentioned stories that were similar to what we have experienced. Sometimes tears would come to my eyes as well as others when fear, problems and situations were mentioned.

Laughter has been exhibited as stories were told of funny things that have happened in church and home life in the "fish bowl." We also have laughed when renewing stories of the past.

The music is fantastic. We are free to express ourselves with praise to God. Voices are raised and the presence of the Lord is felt. Expression of hands raised, eyes to heaven or closed eyes are a welcomed sight.

It is easy to get burned out in the ministry. Children are not encouraged to come. Some may think that this is cruel, but parents need time away occasionally. It is important to take the time to be away from children and to have some time with only a spouse. Also, it is important to be with others in the ministry.

In the years that we have been in the ministry, we have had the privilege of knowing some wonderful ministers and their wives. With concern, we have tried to keep up with families and churches. This conference helps us to do that. The most important thing is that we are renewed and ready to keep on doing what God has called us to do.

Chapter 28

Gone Fishing

ONE BEAUTIFUL WARM DAY in early spring I came home from work. On the front door was a note from Tom. It simply said John 21:3. I was blank as to what the scripture verse said so I went to my Bible and read: "Simon Peter said to them, "I am going fishing" (NIV). I then understood that Tom was doing what he loved. He had gone fishing.

I also love to fish. Many times in our married life we have gone fishing. One church that we were in was located on the Ohio River. A church family invited us to fish on their property. They had a pond and tributaries from the river ran through their land. We spent time with them as a family and enjoyed going to their farm to fish. The association with that family led the man to accept Christ as his Savior.

Where we live now, Tom and I fish in another church member's pond. John and Lou come down to see us sometimes but they have expressed that they know we need the time away. I sit and listen to the cows bawling in the distance and watch the beautiful tall pine trees swaying in the breeze. I could sit for hours listening to the sounds of nature, especially when there is a cool breeze blowing against my face. We have had luck fishing in the pond, most important it is a nice release to just get away from the world and see the beauty that God has made for us to enjoy. We appreciate that we are welcome to share that beauty.

While fishing sometimes you catch fish and other times you don't get a bite. You put out your line in hopes a fish will bite, but sometimes you go home empty-handed. When you haven't had successful day fishing you don't give up altogether. You know that you will catch fish another time. Ministry is the same way. Some people will readily accept you witness and follow the Lord, others will not. You don't give up on people, you realize that a better day is coming and there will be many to share a witness with in the future.

At times, when you are fishing, you realize that you are using the wrong bait or hooks. You change your strategy. Another bait or different size hook are needed. If you are prepared and have the right equipment your chances are better to catch a fish. In ministry, you may need to change your strategy. You never change the gospel, but the method of presenting the gospel may need to be changed.

Tom enjoys catching big fish. I really don't care about the size of the fish. I enjoy seeing the bobber go under the water and pulling up a fish. We have caught many different kinds of fish, big and small. This is the way that we are to view the church. All are wanted and needed in the church. It does not matter what size, age, nationality or sex. All should be welcomed.

We think of the church as the main place to worship. I do also, but some of the most meaningful places that I have worshipped have been sitting on the pond bank. Especially, when the fish are not biting and I am sitting there enjoying the fresh air and beauty all around me. I don't think that this should be an excuse for not attending church. I have heard people say that they never go to church but worship on the golf course, fishing or other sports. Part of worshipping in church is being with other believers, sharing problems and lifting praises to God.

Several years we did not get to go fishing very much, but since the children are grown, we have been able to spend more time on the banks of the pond, river or lake. We enjoy the sport, and being able to get away for a few hours. On a warm sunny day you may hear us say "we have gone fishing."

Chapter 29

Too Much Talking

WE CAN LEARN A lot from our children if we just listen. My son once said to me "I remember that you would spend hours talking, on the phone, to church members about the church problems." He was right. I remembered those days and now ask myself why I was talking to others so much. We would hash things over and over. Maybe I was looking for reassurance that everything was going to be alright and that we had done the right things.

I know that all of us need those in which to confide, to share problems and concerns. We in the ministry get lonely and need others to share concerns. Church members also need other Christians to talk with especially in times of crisis in the church. As well as assurance, the church member needs to understand that God has the ultimate answers.

Sometimes we confide in the wrong people. Discernment is important. We need to learn who has our and the church's best interest in mind. When we need advice, it is important to talk to a person who has proven that they have spiritual wisdom. Friends are important, in and outside of the church. Sometimes friends don't want to hurt feelings and will not give an accurate evaluation of the situation. With wisdom comes the knowledge that the truth needs to be said with love. In the long run, the truth is the best words spoken. We need to learn to accept the evaluation out of love, even if it is not what we want to hear. God will give use the discernment, through prayer, of the action that is needed and understanding of the situation.

Sharing with others is needed, but the greatest need is for more prayer and listening to God speak in any situation. He is the only one who knows the "big picture". He knows our motive as well as others. No one else has all the answers. Less problems would arise if we would talk less and listen more to the Holy Spirit, letting Him guide us to say the right things and make the best decisions.

Chapter 30

Foot Washing

MOST SOUTHERN BAPTIST CHURCHES that I have known do not observe the ordinance of foot washing. As a child I heard of foot washing services but had not been to one. There were comments of the practice in other churches and jokes about not wanting to washing feet especially if they were dirty. It was a practice that was foreign to most Christians that I knew and they did not understand why it was practiced.

Foot washing is biblical. In John chapter 13 Jesus washed his disciples' feet. Verse 13:1 says "Having loved his own who were in the world, he now showed them the full extent of his love" (NIV). Simon Peter asked if Jesus was going to wash his feet. Jesus replied "You do not realize now what I am doing, but later you will understand" John 3:7 (NIV). Jesus humbled himself and gave a gift to those he loved the most. He knew that they would not understand at that time the significance of what he did but would later.

I had not thought much of this observance until early in the 1980s when we took a youth group to Centrifudge (a summer youth conference at Ridgecrest, North Carolina). Our church had nightly devotions after the evening session. On the last night, a young lady shared her experience about the group that she had attended all week. The group opened up and shared things that they had not told anyone else. They shared their struggles and concerns. During the ending session they washed each other's feet. She stated that experience had helped her grow spiritually and that it was one of the most meaningful things that she had ever done.

Later, in another church, I was involved in a Sunday night group meeting. We had been studying foot washing and other ordinance of churches. Those in attendance became close and shared views and concerns. We spent time praying for one another. The group lasted for eight week. This gave us time to know and love each other. On the last night that we met, we paired up and washed another's feet. In the process, we shared our appreciation and love for the other person. The love that we experienced made us all tearful.

Like all observances in the church, it is easy to lose the meaning when it becomes a habit. When we have a special bond with a person it becomes meaningful and unforgettable. We need to show love and humility to others just like Jesus did. There are many ways of showing that love. Foot washing is just one of those ways. The most important thing is that we do what God wants us to do no matter what anyone thinks; we are accountable only to Him.

Chapter 31

Expedient

A DEACON, IN ONE of the churches that we ministered, befriended Tom. He would call Tom frequently and wanted Tom to confide in him. He would come to the church or want Tom to stop by his business. He really seemed to want to be a friend and help his pastor. Until an individual gets to know another it is hard to discern that person's motive.

Some problems arose in the church. This "friend" told Tom that he needed to resign from the church because it was the expedient thing for him to do. When I first heard what was said, I took offense to that statement. I knew what expedient meant but had never thought of it as any reason to resign from a church. I went to the dictionary to read the word's definition. It said "Promoting narrow and selfish interests; pertaining to or prompted by interest rather than by what is right."

Then I went to the Bible and read from Isaiah 42:6 "I the Lord called thee in righteousness, and will l hold thine hand, and will keep thee" (NIV). We knew that this was not the right time to leave. The time would come, years later, but not then.

Why should a pastor leave a church? There are all kinds of reasons to leave. What happened to the will of God for the church as well as the pastor? Most churches have problems from time to time but that in itself is no reason to leave a church. Endurance in a situation helps the pastor as well as the people. It helps to know that God will use both to compromise in a situation for the good.

After that situation, it became apparent that this man was not a friend. His main reason was to try to get information from Tom. He also wanted to control Tom and have him to do what he wanted. When he realized that he could not control him his real motivation showed. What he expected did not happen. He finally left the church with a group that started a new church.

The pastor as well as the church member can find themselves in this situation. We need to guard against others that will lead us a stray and give bad advice. The only way to do that is to pray for direction and discernment. Expedient is a word that should never be considered in staying or leaving a church, only the will of God.

Chapter 32

Insight At The Water Park

WHEN DEBRA WAS STILL in school a water park was built in our town. It was big with all of the newest equipment for playing in water. Debra and a friend from her youth church group wanted to go. It was early August, school was getting ready to start and this was their last chance to go swimming. The weather was extremely hot, but the water was cool. As a child I loved to go to the swimming pool. However, I usually got sunburned. I have an allergy to the sun, which causes me to break out in red bumps and sometimes swell. I decided that I would brave the sun and take them to the water park.

I went prepared. I took sunscreen and several towels to cover myself. Immediately, upon arrival I found a shady spot with an umbrella. It seem like it took me forever to cover myself in sunscreen. Then I realized that the chair that I was sitting in reclined. I had it made.

The girls were having the time of their life. I sat there and watched the other children and their families. It made me happy to see the fun and laughter. The thing that I noticed most was the good time that I was having just observing the crowd. It brought back memories of previous years.

Years earlier after severe depression, I continued to have some anxiety, but never like I had when I was first married. It was hard for me to just sit and enjoy my surroundings. My mind was always thinking and worrying. I had a hard time just relaxing. No matter where I was, I had to be doing something.

That day I sat for hours, praising the Lord with a song in my heart. I felt like all the scriptures, prayers and mental activities that I was taught had become real to me. I realized that spiritually I had and was still maturing, but had made extreme progress. My growth had been gradual. 2 Co 3:18b says that "we are being transformed into his likeness with ever-increasing glory, which comes from the Lord, who is the Spirit" (NIV).

I knew that the prayers that I prayed for years were being fulfilled. I was reminded of Philippians 4:6 "Do not be anxious about anything, but in everything, by prayer and petition, with thanksgiving, present your requests to God" (NIV). I knew that verse for memory, yearning that it be real to me and now it was. My life was being more complete and content.

When the girls got ready to leave, I wanted to stay, but it was closing time. I was at peace with the world. It felt good and refreshed. I finally gathered all my things and left the water park. It was a good day. Afterwards, there have been many days of just sitting and enjoying people without anxiety and worrying. I know that God was in control and I did not have to worry, because He was going to take care of everything.

Chapter 33

The Pastor's Study

ONE NIGHT I WAS waiting in Tom's study for a wedding rehearsal to finish so we could go to the rehearsal dinner. I sat at his desk. My eyes viewed his office. Church members from the present and past had shared with him memorable items. The memories were so vivid and pleasant.

Volumes of books and commentaries stacked the shelves of materials that Tom had studied and used throughout his ministry. His black robe hung on the back of the door. He looks so handsome and regal when he wears that robe, mainly officiating weddings.

Framed on the wall was a beautiful cross-stitched picture showing the date he received his Doctor of Ministry degree. The lady who put hours of work into the picture was proud that her minister worked hard for his accomplishment to serve the Lord. All of his other degrees were framed and hanging on the walls. Each was a reminder of hard work preparing him for the ministry.

An arrangement of silk flowers sat on the windowsill. The flowers were from a funeral of a young lady who died in a car accident. She had babysat our children. Her goal in life was to be a mission volunteer. The flowers were a reminder of her sweet spirit and commitment.

Along with the flowers was a potted plant. Some of the children in Vacation Bible School had given it to Tom. Their love for their pastor was obvious, with big eyes and smiles, as they presented it to him. On his desk was a picture of David and Debra. I examined a picture of myself, taken over thirty years ago when we first married. People do change as they age.

On another wall was a plaque that said "Ye shall be fishers of men." Signed "Jesus" and in the shape of a fish. It was a reminder of our task as Christians. A ceramic statue of a dog listening to an old Victoria with the caption "He hears his Master's voice" had a definite message to the Christian.

Two things especially caught my eyes. First, was a picture called "The Baptizing." It depicted an old country church, a creek beside the church, and a crowd of people. They were watching as two men baptized a woman. The picture was given to us by the parents of a young man who had died in a car accident at seventeen years of age. With all the sadness that we had seen, the picture was a remembrance of new life through the waters of baptism.

Second, a plaque that read "The Pastor's Study". The last few words said "You are always welcomed." The statement could not have been any more correct. Many people had sat in the Pastor's study. Some were heartbroken, sad, with heavy hearts. Others came happy and full of life, expecting great things to happen. Whatever the reason they came; I am assured that they felt loved and welcomed.

Chapter 34

Other Friends In The Ministry

I HAVE HEARD IT said that it is hard for the minister and his wife to have personal friends in the church in which they minister. Sometimes that is true. Selecting those in which to confide can be hard. When there are a lot of family members in the same church it is important to be careful in whom you confide because individuals may be related. It is important to remember when coming into a church that friendships, sometimes life-long friendships, have already been established. You are the outsider and need to prove yourself to have a trustworthy friend.

We all need someone to talk with and share. Sometimes there are other ministers or their wives that you can confide in. Talking about problems is helpful for an outlet to frustrations and concerns. Also, a minister's wives group can be a help. Usually, all have similar problems and need reassurance. When the church has several ministers, they as well as their wives can help each other and listen to each other's particular problems. I know that sometimes this does not work, especially when there are staff problems in the church. The most important thing to remember is that we need each other, but above all we need God. We need to talk with him, share our concerns and burdens and listen to His voice to solve our problems.

Years ago I was a part of a minister's wife group that met once a month. The women shared from their heart. We were made up of all ages, but had common bonds and concerns. When one had a problem we would call and encourage that individual. I know that I felt loved and accepted. We met for five years. Personally, if I could mold a minister's wives group, that would have been the mold. Since then I have attended several other groups. The problem was that they did not last long. Some felt that they did not have the time and others felt that they did not need the support. I was amazed that some said that they never had any problems in their churches. Others spoke as if they had all the answers. I knew that I did not have all the answers and that the fellowship was what I needed.

My life has been made joyful by all of the wonderful church members through the years. I have met and had lasting friendships with many. Proverbs 17:17 "A friend loves at all times" (NIV).

In 1980, Ann needed new carpet for her house. We were new in the church. She asked me to go to Georgia with her and get the carpet. We took her truck and made a two-day trip. We had a wonderful time of laughter and fun. We became friends and while in that church I visited in her home frequently.

Many hours were spent with Susan at her home or ours. She helped me when I needed a friend the most. She helped to pack our things and helped to move us in a bad situation. At one time she was a staff member and many hours were spent in ministry.

Sue and Charlie have been friends for many years. They have been there for us through deaths of loved ones. We would spend time together for meals. On holidays and birthdays we tried to have some special times together.

Sherrie was my exercise buddy until Curves closed down. I was getting over an illness and Sherrie had been sick so we have several things in common. Our fellowship, respect and love for each extend from the church to the community and our families. Debra and I took Sherrie to Nashville to audition for a game show. It was fun just watching her and the excitement she had to be able do something that she really wanted to do. It was a good day. We went on shopping trips where we would spend the night laughing and having fun. It is wonderful to have friends inside and out of the church.

These friendships have been wonderful. After a while, we have gone our separate ways to minister to other churches. After several churches, we learned to accept that as being a part of being in the ministry. We learn that through the years and distance the friendships still last. We may not get to see each other often, but when we do it is just like we haven't been apart.

Chapter 35

Going Home

IN MARCH OF 2000 Tom and I had gone to a chaplain's retreat in Alabama. My father was having a simple procedure in the outpatient clinic at the hospital. When we arrived, I had a message to call home. When I called, I found out that during the procedure that my father's body went into shock and that he was in intensive care. My mother wanted us to stay at the retreat. We were to come back two days later. She said that if he got any worse that she would call. We called frequently and decided to stay.

We left the retreat and went straight to Gallatin, Tennessee, my parent's home. I stayed with mother at the hospital and Tom went home to take care of Debra. That night something happened. The doctors thought that daddy may have had a heart attack. In the middle of the night, they started kidney dialysis. Later, it was decided that he had not had a heart attack, but never knew what had happened.

My father stayed in intensive care for several weeks. Most of the time, he was not aware of his surroundings. Surprisingly, sometimes, he would wake up and know all of us. One day mother and I sat on opposite sides of daddy's hospital bed. Mother would hardly leave daddy, so she was very tired. She laid her head on his bed and fell asleep. Daddy woke up. His hands were restrained because he would pull out his tubes. He looked at me and smiled then he stretched his restrained hand, and patted mother on her head until he fell asleep.

My father had several other procedures but nothing seemed to help. The dialysis was getting harder and harder on his body. His kidney doctor told my mother that he needed to be put in the nursing home. My mother let her know that she had taken care of his mother and she would take care of him.

After consulting with my father's doctor, my mother decided to stop the dialysis. Daddy could not get any better. We knew that he could not live long. My brothers, sisters-in-law, mother and I took care of our father. We brought him home, set up a hospital bed in their den and cared for all of his needs. He had several tubes. We fed him through a tube in his stomach three times a day.

On a Sunday night after feeding daddy, he got very sick. My brothers came. I climbed up in his hospital bed and held him as the boys worked on him. He looked over to us and very plainly he said "I want to go home." We all said that's alright. Hospice told us that people dying sometimes says things like that. We knew what daddy meant. He was already in his earthly home. His life had been lived for the Lord and he was tired. That was the last thing that he said.

The next day, Judy, my sister-in-law, mother and I took care of daddy. He had several visitors. Mother said that daddy needed his hair cut. His barber came. We propped him up in his bed and Mr. Brown gave him a haircut as life went on. Early the next morning, our father died. Through those days, I listened to many people tell about how my father influenced them. How his life was a Christian influence to others. I was proud that he was my father. He had suffered tremendously for the last two months of his life. That was not the important thing, because God never left us through daddy's suffering. The important things were that daddy was faithful to the end and he went home to be with His loving heavenly Father.

Chapter 36

Cancer

In June, 2006 I went for my yearly check-up. I mentioned some of the problems that I was having. The doctor said "your symptoms sound like cancer." That caught my attention. She sent me to get an ultrasound. The ultrasound showed some problems in my uterus, but nothing conclusive. She made an appointment for a specialist. I went to see him. He took biopsies. Tom and I went for the consultation. He said that the biopsies did not indicate cancer, but would not say that cancer was not there. He stated that a Fractional D and C and endometrial ablation were needed.

In August, I had the procedure. Two days later, the doctor called to say that I had cancer of the endometrial lining of the uterus. He sent me to an oncologist at Vanderbilt Medical Center in Nashville, Tennessee. On August 30, 2006 I had exploratory surgery, a complete hysterectomy taking lymph nodes.

The surgery was a success. The lymph nodes were clear. The cancer had gone only into 10% of the endometrial lining, giving me a good prognosis without the need of any treatments. When I went for my first check-up the doctor stated that my first two years were the most important and that I needed to come back every three months.

There were over two months between the time that cancer was first mentioned and it was confirmed. When we hear "cancer" the normal concern is "how long do I have to live?" During that time I thought of Tom, my children, my mother and mother-in-law. The things that stayed on my mind were the things that I knew that the Lord wanted me to do and the things that were left undone. There was an urgency to complete those things.

When I received the news that I was over 90% cancer-free, I felt that God was giving me more time to complete His work and that I needed to get busy. I am a positive person but also a realist. I know that no doctor can be 100% sure of a cure and that I may have cancer again. I will not spend my time dwelling on that fact, but rather focus on what I need to do. The feeling of urgency gave me that boost.

Facing my mortality was an advantage. Those who don't face the fact that death can come in a short period of time or instantly, sometimes live as if they have forever. They think that they will have plenty of time to do what needs to be done. In actuality, that may not be true.

I know a lot of people with cancer or critical illnesses but not until then did I completely understand the ups and downs. I understood the concerns for the future and how it could affect families. It now became personal. I felt guilty. I received a good report, but several friends did not get a good report. I wanted to listen to them, pray for them and help bear their burdens. I had experienced some of the same feelings that they were dealing with and I knew how the unknown felt.

In the churches we have served, there are two people that I remember the most and their battle with cancer. One was Lorene. She was a church secretary that we were privileged to know and minister with. She fought the disease for years and with many treatments. During her illness she or her husband Clyde did not waiver in their faith and commitment to the Lord. The second was our friend Charlie. He was one of the most loving caring Christian that I have ever known. In September 2006, he had melanoma.

After surgery he was told he was cancer-free. In September 2007, it came back and in a matter of a month he was gone. He loved the Lord and it was obvious the way he lived his life.

My mother-in-law got sick in May 2009. She was diagnosed with lung cancer. We kept her at home as long as we could. When it became impossible for us to care for her we had to put her in a Nursing Facility. My brother-in-law, Buddy, Tom and I took turns daily going to the Nursing Facility to be with her and make sure she knew we were there for her. She fought for four months and was surrounded by her family as she left this life to be with her heavenly father.

In August, 2012 cancer struck again as Buddy got sick. He had moved back to Florida to be near his sons. He was also diagnosed with lung cancer. He had surgery to remove a tumor and never recovered from the surgery. In September we buried another family member from cancer.

None of us know the length of our life, but cancer does get an individual's attention. Our thoughts start to put things into perspective. The things that need to be done, the words not spoken, our families and friends and above all when we die where we are going. For the Christian that destiny has already been decided and God will be waiting to receive us. There is never a better time than today to accept him as our Savior and start living doing the things that we are called to do. Cancer can take a person out of this world, but so can many other things and none of us know how long we have to live.

Chapter 37

Love Returned

It was Thursday June 14, 2007 that my mother had a stroke. The day was extremely hot. She had gone to the mail box, turned around and fell. For several years she had problems with her right knee. She thought that her knee caused her to fall.

Three of my brothers and their families live near my mother. None were home or near since all work and were at their jobs. Usually the police patrolled that area during the day. It was common for mother, while tending the garden, to see them as they passed by, but not that day. Mother did not know the length of time that she laid in the hot sun, but it seemed like hours to her.

She scooted to the house, while my nephew's basset hound kept her company. Buster never left her side. While she rested from her long journey to the house, Buster laid his head on her chest. She managed to scoot inside the house. There she waited for one of my brothers to come by while going home from work. When my brothers arrived at her house they tried to get her to go to the emergency room. She refused to go, continuing to think that her knee was the problem. She had an appointment with her orthopedist the next month and thought it could wait and that her knee would get better in a few days.

My family was in eastern Kentucky attending Debra's graduation from training school. The next day, I received a call from my brother Johnny. He told me about the fall and that mother would not go to the doctor. He also said that she was having problems getting around. My brothers even went out and bought her motorized scooter, thinking that she could operate it and get around better. That morning they had taken her to the beauty shop to get her hair set and had to lift her in and out of the chair. I told Johnny that as soon as we got back to our home in Kentucky, I would leave and come to Tennessee.

That evening when we got home, I called mother. I spoke with her. She told me about the incident. As the day progressed her ambulation had gotten worse. Then she said "I think that I have had a stroke." Before mother retired, she worked in the hospital and knew all the symptoms. By then she was ready to go to the hospital. But she wanted to wait till I got there. Mother always thought that all her children had certain duties and mine was to take her to the hospital.

Early the next morning, I got her ready, my brother Jerry picked mother up and put her in the car and we went to the hospital. We waited all day in the emergency room. Finally after 8 hours she was put in a room. They told me that she had a mild stroke. By the next morning her right side was showing the effects of a stroke. The right side of her mouth started to droop. Mother stayed several weeks in the hospital. The doctor had a meeting with my brother, Carl, and sister-in-law, Sue. The doctor told then that she had a major stroke and the prognosis was not good.

Mother needed physical therapy in hopes that she might regain some use of her right side, so my brothers took her to a nursing facility. Mother was always the one to take care of everyone else. It was hard for her to have others taking care of her. While in the nursing home she told me "when I go home, I am going to make a pretzel salad and bring back to the girls." That was one of the favorite recipes she made and shared with others.

As the days went by, mother did not show much progression. Our family met several times, discussing mother's health and the future. My brother Tim and his family would come from Alabama on the weekends. We did not know what was going to happen, but we made decisions as a family, the siblings and spouses. Mother wanted to go home. We decided after she completed rehabilitation we were going to bring her home and hire sitters to care for her. We wanted the best for mother and if that meant using all her money and selling the farm for her care that is what we decided to do.

Then her health worsened and something happened. She was taken to the hospital for test. The doctors never did say that mother had another stroke but she lost her ability to swallow. Mother could not move by herself and could not eat or drink. She would need a feeding tube. She said that she did not want a feeding tube. She required total care. We asked her several times about the feeding tube, but she continued to refuse. She had a living will and she made it clear to us about her wishes. We discussed with mother what would happen without the feeding tube. Mother voiced that she understood. She lost all use of her body. Physical therapy was not working. Our mother no longer could help others and for her that was devastating.

The nursing home was going to make mother comfortable and let nature take its course. Again, we met as a family. My sister-in-laws, Judy and Sue said that mother wanted to go home and thought that we needed to bring her home. I will always be grateful that they spoke up that day and said what they did. At that time, I was not thinking about what mother wanted as much as thinking that the nursing home could provide the best care for her. We started making phone calls looking for an agency that could provide needed care for mother at home. Home-in-stead senior care was hired and we brought mother home. Hospice also started coming in to see mother. They told us that she would probably live no longer than two weeks.

The agency came from 7:00am till 7:00pm. However, one of us was usually there to help with mother's care. At least one of us would stay at night. The last week and a half I went to my mother's home to stay until she died. At night, our family would have supper together. Her church family and friends would bring food and we would cook. We tried to make things as normal as possible. It was a difficult time, but a good time. Carter, mother's great grandchild got in bed with mother and talked with her. We don't know what they discussed but that was a special time for her. She loved her family and being with us.

Our family did not have anyone with medical training. Most of the time, we felt like "fish out of water." We did not want to hurt mother but we were not skilled caring for a very sick person. The Lord sent an angel our way. Her name is Shannon. At the time she was our nephew, Jeremiah's fiancé. Shannon is a nurse. She would come every night and help us and give us some pointers of what to do.

My birthday was on a Saturday. Our whole family had gathered. They gave me a birthday party. We have a lot of children in our family. My brother, Carl brought over his four-wheeler. The children took turns riding and playing together. Afterwards, the adults gathered around mother's bed and released our mother to go be with our dad. We all spoke to her. We wanted her to know that we would be alright and that we loved her, thanking her for all the wonderful years she had given us as our mother. Then we cried.

The third week started, mother continued to get weaker but totally aware of everything. Hospice told use that when a person hangs on that it may be that there is something left undone. Mother and I talked a lot at night time. After several days and many prayers, I felt that mother was hanging on for us. She loved the Lord and wanted to go to heaven, but she also loved us and still wanted to be with her family. On Friday night, she went to sleep holding my hand. During the night, she would wake and reach for my hand. This went on all night. The next day, my brothers and sisters-in-law got to the house early. I was exhausted and later in the day I took a nap. They had told us that people usually die at night or early morning hours. Mother's condition for the last few days seemed to be the same, so I decided to go to one of the local stores to get out of the house for a while. While I was out, I received a call from Judy to say that mother's blood pressure was dropping. I finished up and got home. When I entered the house I knew it would not be long. Judy, looked at me, and said "she is waiting for you." It was not long afterwards that mother took her last breath.

She died on Saturday afternoon and we buried her on Monday. There was no big hurry but we had been with mother for weeks and had completed all the plans just like she wanted. Everything had been done. Before the funeral, our family met for a prayer around her casket. As we held hands and prayed, a video was showing pictures of our family on a screen in the background. Several people mentioned to me about the love that they saw in our family.

It was a beautiful warm sunny September day at the cemetery. The birds were chirping and appeared that all was right with the world. At the closing of the grave, my brothers and nephews shoveled the dirt over mother's coffin, just like they did when my father died. It was a gesture of love. The day was a reminder that life goes on and all was right with the world because the Lord was still in control.

I miss my mother. We loved to cook and shop together. But I would not want her back like she was and I did not want her to suffer any longer. My memories of both my parents are wonderful, but it was time for us to let go of them. I hope that from mother I have inherited the strong will to be a supportive person that is loyal and shows great love. From my father, I pray that I have the love and compassion that he had for all people. From both, I pray that I have the commitment that they had to each other and to God. I feel that both live in me. I am thankful that God saw fit to put me in the family that he did. One thing that I know is that we tried to give back to both parents a little of what they gave to us. They instilled many things in us but the one thing that we knew was that we were loved. When both got sick, we had to return that love. True love requires that we return love. Just like when Jesus came to earth to die for us, it was out of love. If we have accepted Him as Savior, we have the desire to follow Him and return the love to Him, our parents, family and our fellow mankind.

Chapter 38

Family

As well as loving Tom, Debra, David and Gretchen, I love my extended family. My brothers: Johnny, Jerry, Carl and Tim hold a special place in my heart. Through the years each has shown a strong faith and commitment to the Lord. My brothers have different personalities, talents and physical features. I admire each for their uniqueness. When I was grown, someone asked me if I regretted not having a sister. I said "no" I did not know any difference and they were the best brothers that a sister could have.

My sisters-in-law: Judy, Sue, Nancy and Gloria are special to me. They help our family to stay close. Years ago when we were without a church and Christmas was approaching, we received money. It came from a family member(s). I know that my sister(s)-in-law were responsible for the gift. The money allowed us to go home for the holidays and have money for gifts. Our children have learned the value of a close family connection. Each family member was there for our parents, each doing what was needed. We looked forward to getting together for holidays and other family events.

Tom's family is the same way. Most of his family lives out of state. In the last years, we have been able to get together more and enjoy those times. One particular time his whole family met at his sister Rhonda's lake house. His mother and all of her children and grandchildren were there. We enjoyed outings, fishing, boating but most of all just being together. We just wish we could see them more often.

For several years my mother-in-law lived by herself in Bowling Green, Kentucky. It was an hour from our house, but also the town in which my job was located. Before her son moved in to help care for her I would stay with her during the week. We would cook, shop and enjoy each other's company. That is the same way that it should be with the church. We need to love being together and enjoy each other's company. We are a family, the family of God. The church is made up of people with different talents and personalities. All are important and each has something to offer. Not one person is more important than another. Each member should be treated with respect and accepted for who they are.

We need to visit and care for each other. When a church member cries, we need to cry with them. When they laugh, we need to laugh. No matter how insignificant we think a situation is, it is important to the individual and we should always show concern for them. When the individuals in the church learn to love and cherish each other in spite of differences, then the church will become a family like God intended. We will enjoy being together and others will know we have something that they desire. They will want to be a member of our church family.

Chapter 39

Living And Dying

WE ATTENDED THE FUNERAL of a pastor of our Hispanic ministry. Several days after having heart surgery he had a major heart attack and died. He had a zeal and love for people which was obvious. He was only forty-two years old, with a wife and two small children. His funeral was a celebration. The music and words spoken were uplifting and a testimony of his faith, life and commitment. His wife gave a heartfelt testimony of praise to the Lord.

I was reminded of all of the many funerals that I have attended. The reactions of the family are many. Of course there is grief, but sometimes the grief is unnatural. It is as if there are a lot of unresolved feelings. Sometimes the ones who grief the hardest are those that have guilt. Guilt because there are things left undone, words left unspoken and words that should not have been spoken. It is difficult to accept that a loved one or friend is gone and will not be seen again. It is natural to feel the loss and grief.

When I was in senior high, a classmate suddenly died. She was going to be a missionary. The cause of death was a blood clot to the brain. I started thinking about death and why some who have so much to offer die young. I also noticed that some people who never do anything seem to live a long life.

In college, the dean of student's wife had her fifth child. Shortly afterward, she was diagnosed with cancer and given six months to live. During that time, I listened to her testimony twice. She was confident that God would care of her family and that if she lived that was fine, but she said that if she died that would be alright. She knew that God would take care of her family. I prayed that God would heal her. He did not.

An infant was thrown from the vehicle her mother was driving. She was fastened in a car seat properly. The strap broke and the car seat was thrown from the car. She lived a short time. The family grieved over her tiny casket. Her mother had such guilt, but could not have done anything any different. She asked: "Why did this have to happen?"

My first teaching job was teaching birth to three-year-old handicapped children. The first year I lost three of the children that I taught. Even with severe handicaps, they were very special children with so much love to give and receive. God had placed them with their families, maybe for a short time, but for a reason.

There have been numerous children and teenagers in our churches that have died. Some had long-term illness and others died suddenly. A child's death is always difficult. The death that was extremely hard for Tom was the death of a child who had a brain tumor. He and Candy talked for hours. She may have been a 12-year-old, but she had spiritual knowledge much older. We had a healing service for her and her family. It may sound strange, but the service helped her family to accept that she was not going to live but be permanently healed. The service was what they needed to help them through her last days and death.

When David was a teenager, he had several friends to die in car accidents. During a five year period, six friends died. Most were accidents that had nothing to do with speed or alcohol. Holes in the pavement, fog and losing control of the car were the cause of the accidents. Out of love, David and some friends dug one of their friend's grave. That was one way that these young men expressed their love for a friend. When young people die we often say: "They had their whole lives ahead of them."

My father and father-in-law died in the same year. My father had suffered tremendously two months before he died. My father-in-law had Alzheimer's. He was not the man that he once was. He was tired of the disease. He did not know what was happening to him, but knew that he wasn't the same. When they died, we were thankful that they did not have to suffer anymore, both knew their destination.

I have seen God heal people and I know that he is in the healing business. But God does not always choose to heal and He does not always keep accidents from happening and life spared. I have learned that it is in God's hands and that he has a reason for healing and sparing. He also has a reason for death and illnesses. Some of the most effective testimonies that I have heard have been from those who were not healed or have gone through terrific grief. Yet, they have a strength that only God can give and their lives are an inspiration to others.

Dying is a process of life and grief can be overwhelming no matter the age. The way we grieve when someone we love dies shows the world what we think about life and dying. Above all, who we believe in and where our strength comes from. As well as living our lives, the world looks at how we response to death. Does our grieving reflect our beliefs? Do we know that our love one is going to a better place? Do we know that God will comfort and give us the strength to go on?

The greatest grief that I have suffered is the unexpected death of my youngest brother Tim. I love all my brothers but Tim was the one I had the privilege of caring for when he was a child. There was ten years difference in our age and mother gave me the responsibility of caring for him. He thought that I could not love another person but him and when I married he was not happy. He was only fourteen years old at the time, but he got over it when he grew up and fell in love. He went to college, married and moved out of state. Our family is close and his family always came home at least two times a year when we had family events or other times to visit mother.

After some very difficult years, in 2014 Tim committed suicide. My family knows all the details and it is not important that others know what happened. The important thing is that through the days, weeks and years since that time, God has been with us and given us the strength that we need. The first week of his death, all I could do was to rest in Jesus' arms and let him carry me. I was overtaken with tremendous grief and sadness.

God has taken care of his wife and three daughters. Their church has been there to help in many ways. Their daughters have flourished in colleges and high school. Tim was a Christian and he and Nancy instilled in their children to live for Christ. I know that Tim would be proud of the life his children are living and the wonderful mother Nancy has been to their daughters. When I look at the girls, I can see Tim living in them. It has been hard and they have overcome many obstacles, but God has given them and the rest of our family the strength and love that we needed to go through that difficult time and continues to give us the strength that we need.

Chapter 40

Patience

In September, 2008 Tom asked his family doctor to look at his nose. He had a small place that had previously opened up and bled. His physician said that he did not think that the place was anything but he would send him to a specialist. In October, he went for his appointment. Again, the specialist said that he did not think that the place was of concern but he decided to take a biopsy. The biopsy was positive. Tom was scheduled for minor surgery in the doctor's office. He went for the surgery. The doctor operated twice but said that there was still more cancer. He had several types of skin cancer. Tom had to officiate at a funeral that afternoon and had to get back for the funeral service. He was told to come back to the doctor's office the next morning for more surgery. He did and the doctor said that he felt that he needed to wait until Tom's nose healed before cutting on it again. When he went back, his nose was infected and had to wait until after he completed his antibiotics.

On Tuesday December 2, 2008 I took Tom to have more surgery. The procedure is called NOHS. A small part of the infected skin is cut out, the incision is stitched or bandaged and the patient waits to hear from the test results. If there is more cancer, the doctor starts the procedure again. Each time he shoots the nose with a local anesthesia which deadens the affected area. That day, he had three surgeries and was told that more cancer was found. His local doctor said that the kind of basil cell cancer Tom had was a "monster." He said that it was time for Tom to go to Louisville to a doctor who specialized in the NOHS surgeries. However, he said that it probably would be in January before he could get Tom an appointment.

Within thirty minutes, we got a call from Louisville asking us to come on Thursday of that week. We were to bring clothes to stay if needed. Early Thursday morning we arrived to see Dr. McCall. The doctor performed two surgeries that day; he said that there was more cancer. We stayed in a motel within a block of the clinic so we would be close. We had to be at the clinic early the next morning.

The weather was cold and Tom had a big bandage on his nose which made it hard for him to see. He could not wear his contacts or glasses. I dropped him off at the door of the clinic and parked the car. I went into the office, looked around to fine Tom and noticed that he was talking to a beautiful young lady. I sat down beside of him and he said "Do you remember Ralph and Marcella? This is Kim, their daughter." Kim was a small child in one of our churches years before. We had not seen her since we left the church. She had taken her mother-in-law to have a similar surgery. She heard the receptionist call Tom's name. When he sat down, she asked him if he was a minister. She told him who she was and that she vaguely remembered us but had heard her parents, many times, talk about us.

During that day, Tom had five surgeries. The stress of the large number of shots caused him some trauma. The nurses kept Tom back in one of the operating rooms instead of letting him go out with the others. I spent my time with Tom and sitting with Kim. We discussed the church and members. She caught me up and everything that had happened for years. Her mother-in-law was told that they had gotten the cancer and she was waiting to get stitched and go home. We stayed there until they closed. They did not have the results of the fifth surgery, because the pathologists had gone home. We were told to come back on Monday morning.

During the weekend, Kim called to check on Tom. I told her of the plans. She asked that we come back on Sunday and stay with her and her family. We hesitated, but decided that it would be better to go on Sunday afternoon instead of early Monday morning. When a minister has lived in the same state and in many different towns, it is not uncommon to run into people that you know. We visited with Kim and her husband Rick. Not only did we have our faith in common but we discovered that we had other interest. It was a reminder that where ever we go there are those who we know and have common bonds and that God puts people in our lives to be a blessing when we need it most.

The next morning, we went back to the clinic. The last surgery was still not clear. By that time, Tom was getting anxious. He had so much numbing medicine that it did not seem to be effective anymore. They took more cancerous skin. This time it came back clear. That afternoon, they started the skin grafts. His entire nose had to be grafted. Two doctors took four to six inches of skin from both shoulders for the grafts. It took all afternoon to complete the grafts.

During most of the grafting, I stayed in the waiting room. I had been in the room with him for most of the surgeries. At that point he was in tremendous pain. There was not anything that I could do and I felt that I was getting in the way of the three nurses and two doctors. While in the waiting room I listened to the others complaining about having to wait so long to be stitched or have another surgery. Most of those waiting lived in Louisville area. I knew that they had to wait because the doctors were working on Tom. However, with the kind of surgeries that they performed it was not uncommon to have several surgeries on one person during the day and cause the schedule to run late.

After three hours of listening to the complaining, I very softly said, "I understand the long wait. My husband and I have been here for the last three days from starting time to closing. He has had a total of 14 surgeries on his nose. This afternoon, he is having his entire nose grafted. When they are finished, I have to drive him three hours to get home." Everyone was quiet for a while.

When the doctors were finishing, Tom asked the doctor about the graft and reconstruction surgery. He stated that he did not want to reconstruct Tom's nose at that time, maybe in a year. He said "We got all the cancer that we saw, but I don't know that we got all that was there." Tom was raised in Florida. The sun had damaged his skin as a child. That was the cause of his skin cancers. Dr. McCall did say that if they had not aggressively completed the surgeries that Tom probably would have lost his nose. He was released back to his previous doctor for the follow-up.

For several weeks Tom had problems with his nerves. His doctor told him that he suffered from the same symptoms that people who are tortured. The pain and nervousness would go away within time. Also, if they had known the extent of his cancers they probably would have put him to sleep. Slowly, he started to get better.

Tom had to go back each week to see the doctor in Bowling Green, KY, which was only an hour from our home. He was told that part of his skin graft took, but part of it did not. Tom's skin graft had several layers. The doctor started cutting away the bad skin and sometimes finding good skin. The doctor did say that if he needed to graft skin again that he was going to put Tom asleep for the surgery and he would not have the trauma he had before. That pleased Tom. We knew that it was still going to be a long recovery. His resistance was low and he had to be careful not to catch anything.

Right before New Year's Day Tom started getting sick and went to see his regular doctor. He was put on another antibiotic. After two weeks his health continued to get worse. I took him to the hospital and he was admitted. He was gasping for breath. He stayed five days with pneumonia and bronchitis. His recuperation took several weeks. This delayed the cutting away of dead skin.

During that time, we felt very blessed to be in the church we were in. Some deacons and church members got out of their comfort zone and did things they had never done before to make sure that ministry continued. They were considerate of us and our situation and gave Tom time to heal.

When I thought back to all that had transpired I was reminded of the day in the waiting room with the complainers. Since I was there several hours I wrote down the comments that some had made but it came down to the fact that people are impatient. We do not like to wait because we all have things to do that we think are important. An inconvenience makes us late or not able to do the things that we plan and we lose our patience.

For us, this has turned into a time of learning more patience. We don't know if they got all of the cancers. We do know that there are probably more surgeries. It is going to take months and maybe years for the total reconstruction of Tom's nose. Patience is a hard lesson, but we have to learn to endure the unexpected, relax and know that God is still in control. Verses that have and are helping me are from Romans 12:12 "Be joyful in hope, patient in affliction, faithful in prayer" (NIV) and Col 1:11 "Being strengthened with all power according to his glorious might so that you may have great endurance and patience" (NIV). I hope that we never forget that the Bible holds truths that we can hold onto especially in our time of greatest need.

Chapter 41

The Grace Of God

GRACE IS DIVINE HELP or favor. I am reminded of the many times that God extends His grace to us. Sometimes we were aware of that grace; other times we did not know, at the time, that he intervened in our lives and kept disaster from happening.

Grace was there when as a young bride depression consumed my life. He provided the counseling that was needed and a husband who was patient and loving.

Grace was there when the young man's car crossed in front of me. My car was totaled. The young man did not have a scratch. I had minor problems with my shoulders that physical therapy corrected.

Grace was there when the bull crossed the country road right in front of my car. The Lord took the stirring wheel to go right behind him, without hurting him, Tom or myself.

Grace was there when we were without a church for one and a half years. He brought people into our lives to encourage and help us get through a very difficult time.

Grace was there when the doctor told us that our infant son was a few hours from death because he was so ill. He stayed days in the hospital, isolated, because his immune system was so low. With love and prayers he made it.

Grace was there the day that Tom fell down an earthen dam. He and our son, David, were fishing and decided to take a short cut. Tom stepped on a rock, it shifted, and he fell twenty feet on rocks. He hurt his spine. He was hospital twice and was told that it was a miracle that he could walk.

Grace was there to help our son work through some difficult times on his spiritual journey. God kept him in His hands until he could see his way back.

Grace has been there to help us with the understanding and helping our daughter, Debra. To help us find the school that she needed and continue to help her find her place in work and church.

Grace was there to comfort through the death of my father, mother, father-in-law, mother-in-law, brother-in-law and youngest brother. He gave us the strength to be there and comfort each other through the process of dying and grief.

Grace was with us when we waited for several months of testing to find out that I had cancer. After surgery, came the words "You are cancer-free."

Grace has been with us through fourteen surgeries for skin cancer on Tom's nose.

Grace will be with us in retirement as we continue to serve Him.

God's grace has been through all the pain and hardships. One of these days through the process of death or His coming again grace will lead us home to be with Him.

Hebrews 4:16 says "Let us then approach the throne of grace with confidence, so that we may receive mercy and find grace to help us in our time of need" (NIV).

Chapter 42

My Prayer For The Church Member

I HAVE LEARNED A great respect for church members. I think that there are a lot of problems that could be avoided with more time praying and less time talking. The church, as well as the minister, needs prayer. My prayers for the church are:

1. To love the pastor and other ministerial staff and their families. Accepting them for their unique talents.

2. To realize that each is different and not to compare them to previous ministers. To be aware that each minister has his faults, nobody is perfect. After all there are no perfect people.

3. To pray for instead of criticizing your minister. He has a greater chance of changing, bathed in prayers.

4. To not expect the minister's children to be saints. They are just children and will make mistakes like your children.

5. To respect the minister's home, even if he does live in a parsonage. It is their place of residence. That is where he and family are making a home and that needs to be respected.

6. When the minister needs advice, give it with love, compassion and concern.

7. When the minister leaves, let him go. Do not hang on to him or his family. You can and should remain friends. This is sometimes very hard, especially when a church member and the minister have been extremely close. He as well as you should look forward to the future and new relationships.

8. When the church has dissensions, be a part of the solution, not the problem. Help your minister with prayer and support.

9. To be committed to the Lord first, then the church. Everything will then fall into place.

When the church member prays more and wants the church to be what God meant it to be then the church and the minister can have a healthy, spiritual relationship.

Chapter 43

My Prayer For The Minister's Wife

THERE ARE SEVERAL PRAYERS for the minister's wife. We must learn that we cannot become the minister's wife that we need to be without prayer and action. My prayers are:

1. To accept that all the people in the church are important. Age, sex, race, income or position in society make no difference. All are important to God and need to know that they are loved. We may feel a calling to work with a certain group, that is fine, but we must never make some feel that they are not accepted.

2. To be willing to go where God leads you and your spouse. To accept God's calling and to support your spouse. Accept his weakness and faults, knowing that you also have weaknesses and faults. Pray with and encourage your spouse through the good and bad times.

3. To accept that you are limited in what you can do. You are just like everyone else. You can't do everything in the church even though you may be expected to do so. Find your talents

and use them. Accept your weaknesses and do not compare yourself to other minister wives. You are unique to God.

4. When being in a church where there are other ministers and their families to learn to work together. To listen to fellow wives' concerns and problems. Accept them and know that they are struggling just like you. When asked for your opinion, give it with love and tact. Accept other wives as you would want to be accepted.

5. Encourage your children to accept and follow Christ. When our faith is important to us we will be an example to our children in the way that we live. Never be afraid to say "I am sorry" when we have blown it. Help them to understand that not all Christians act as Christians. We are not responsible for the way someone else acts, but only for our actions. Encourage them to learn to forgive as well as accept forgiveness. Help them to learn to love and accept being loved. Teach them to seek God's will for their life and not choose that will for them.

6. To grow in faith knowing that God will provide. Just because things are not going well does not mean that God is not there. This is when we should lean on Him and within time, we will see that He has brought us through. Faith can grow through difficulty if we allow it to. God will carry you through problems and heartaches. You will be lifted to the mountaintop as you see Him work.

7. To love the people in each church. Not fearing to get close, but knowing that the length of time being with them may be limited. When it is time to leave, it is important to encourage church members to love the next minister and his family. It is human nature to hold onto people but you need to let go. This does not mean that you stop your friendship, but allow church members to love other ministers and their families.

8. Above all, I pray that you will grow in wisdom to share with others and be an inspiration to those with which you come in contact. Then, the church member will know that you love them and that love is because of your commitment to the Lord.

Chapter 44

The Final Chapter

YEARS AGO, I FELT impressed to write. I had put thoughts down for years, but did not feel that I had the ability. My writing is out of obedience to the Lord. When I became sick, the Lord impressed on me that it was time. I am not an expert of the Bible, I am a shepherd's wife. Through the years, my knowledge has come from studying the Bible, praying, listening to other Christians and trying to be the best minister's wife that I was capable of being. I have fallen short at times through the years. God has always helped me to realize my failures and needs. But through His grace and help I have had the strength to come this far and stayed committed to His calling for my life.

My purpose for writing is to share with other minister's wives as well as all those on a spiritual journey. For those who have not accepted Christ as their Savior, I would like to encourage anyone to take that step. Life will be more fulfilling, satisfying and exciting that one could ever imagine. I personally would not ask for anything more than to have Christ living in me daily and heaven when I die. My desire is also to help those who are struggling and to encourage them to know that others have and are going through similar situations. To gain faith to know that we are never alone, that God is always near even when he is not felt.

If I knew what I know now, would I have started this journey? Yes, I would do it again, but I would have done some things differently. I would take the bad with the good, the discouragement with the encouragement, and the pain with the joy without complaining. Without the bad times, we would not enjoy the good times. Spiritual growth does not happen if we always have things go our way and are on the mountain top. We grow when we are tested and have to prove our faith. God does not always approve of the things that happen in life or how people treat us, but He will use those things to help us grow. We can become better people because of those situations if we chose to learn from them and depend on God.

I also have a love for the church member. Many friendships have been made and will last for a lifetime. I have met some of the most loving and courageous people. They have loved us and through their commitment have inspired our Christian faith and helped us to keep going.

Philippians 3:13–14 "Brothers, I do not consider myself yet to have taken hold of it. But one thing I do: Forgetting what is behind and straining toward what is ahead, I press on toward the goal to win the prize for which God has called me heavenward in Christ Jesus" (NIV). It has been a marvelous journey. Where that journey continues to lead, God's grace will give us the strength to follow. Many years, many miles and much love have followed us through these years. I don't know what the future holds, but I know who holds the future and that is enough.

www.ingramcontent.com/pod-product-compliance
Lightning Source LLC
LaVergne TN
LVHW011945070526
838202LV00054B/4801